Jl 22 '91	8 Ag '94		
26 Ag '91	23 Fe '98		
16 Se '91	6 Ma '00		
30 Se '91	20 N '00		
18 No '91			
16 De '91			
27 Ja '92			
29 Ju '92			
10 Ag '92			
8 Se '92			

Books by Barbara Corcoran

A Dance to Still Music
The Long Journey
Meet Me at Tamerlain's Tomb
A Row of Tigers
Sasha, My Friend
A Trick of Light
The Winds of Time
All the Summer Voices
The Clown
Don't Slam the Door When You Go
Sam
This Is a Recording
Axe-time, Sword-time
Cabin in the Sky
The Faraway Island
Make No Sound
Hey, That's My Soul You're Stomping On
"Me and You and a Dog Named Blue"
Rising Damp
You're Allegro Dead
A Watery Grave
August, Die She Must
The Woman in Your Life
Mystery on Ice
Face the Music
A Horse Named Sky
I Am the Universe
The Hideaway
The Sky Is Falling
The Private War of Lillian Adams
The Potato Kid
Annie's Monster
Stay Tuned

STAY TUNED

Barbara Corcoran

A Jean Karl Book

Atheneum   1991   New York

Collier Macmillan Canada
TORONTO
Maxwell Macmillan International Publishing Group
NEW YORK   OXFORD   SINGAPORE   SYDNEY

Atheneum
Macmillan Publishing Company
866 Third Avenue
New York, NY 10022

Collier Macmillan Canada, Inc.
1200 Eglinton Avenue East
Suite 200
Don Mills, Ontario M3C 3N1

First Edition
Printed in the United States of America
10   9   8   7   6   5   4   3   2   1
Designed by Kimberly M. Hauck

Library of Congress Cataloging-in-Publication Data

Corcoran, Barbara,
    Stay tuned / Barbara Corcoran.— 1st ed.
        p.   cm.
    Summary: En route to stay with a relative she has never seen,
fourteen-year-old Stevie meets three other young people with no
place to live and takes a detour with them into a new life in the
New Hampshire woods.
        ISBN 0–689–31673–9
        [1. Runaways—Fiction.   2. New Hampshire—Fiction.]   I. Title.
PZ7.C814Ss   1991
[Fic]—dc20
90–1017

To Marcia Dunn, skipper of the Peagreen Boat,
home port KUFM, Missoula, Montana, and to
her crew and her devoted followers

Chapter 1

STEVIE HUDDLED ON THE NARROW COT WITH HER FEET pulled up under her, the baseball bat held tight in her hand. She thought she had heard a rat, but it was a huge cockroach that scuttled across the floor. Her father said there weren't any rats here, but she knew better; she had seen one, right here in this disgusting room. That was when she bought the bat.

She looked at her watch for the hundredth time. Her father was later than usual. She hoped he wasn't in some bar. He never used to have more than a sociable beer with his friends, when they were in Iowa, but when her mother died three years ago, he brought home the first of the bourbon bottles. You couldn't drink too much too often and take care of a big farm. It wasn't till he lost the farm to the bank, and he and Stevie left Iowa and came to New York, that it got really bad for a while.

She heard someone screaming out in the hall. She shuddered and looked at the door chain to make sure it was fastened, although she knew it was. There was a lot of

1

screaming and terrible weeping in this hotel. Her father said it had been a luxury hotel once, but that must have been a hundred years ago. The wallpaper was stained and faded, and the one window in their room opened on an air shaft and was streaked with dirt. The whole place smelled terrible.

"It's just for a short spell," her father said. They had come to New York because he had been here for a year when he was a young man and he thought of it as familiar, but he had been dismayed at how changed it was. Times Square—she could remember how he used to describe New Year's Eve in Times Square. It was one of the first places he took her, but it was all porno shops and sleazy, scary-looking places, and the people pushed you right off the sidewalk if you got in their way. Stevie had been terrified.

"I guess things have changed," her father said. "But I'll have me a job in no time, and we'll live in the suburbs somewhere. The East has more jobs than they can get people for." He had counted on an old college friend whose address on East Forty-eighth Street he had hung on to for years, but when they went over there, the brownstone where this friend had lived was gone.

For a week they stayed in a cheap motel. Stevie was afraid to go out alone while her father went job-hunting, and anyway she didn't know how to get anywhere, so she stayed in the dingy room, reading and trying not to be scared. It was a new experience, this terror. At home she had thought of herself as fairly competent. She could drive a tractor and milk a cow and help a cow calve. She could work all day in the cornfield at harvest time. Sometimes something frightened her, like the time lightning struck the barn when she was in it, or the time their old horse cornered her up against the fence and would have crushed her if her father hadn't come along. But things like that were nothing compared to the cold, continuing fear that stayed with her all the time here.

They had had to leave the motel because it cost too much. Somebody in a bar had told her father about this hotel, which was a little cheaper. It was in the West Thirties, which saved her father subway fare, but that was all you could say for it. A lot of welfare people lived here, prostitutes hung around downstairs, and drug dealers roamed the halls and stairways. Today she had had to go out to the deli to get some food, and a filthy old man with long white hair had grabbed her. She had to hit him to get away. Luckily she was big for fourteen, and the farm had given her muscles. She ran all the way back to the hotel and up the three flights of stairs. She knew better than to take the elevator, where you could get trapped with some creep.

She got off the bed now, making sure the cockroach had disappeared, and got the bag of pretzels from the tiny refrigerator. It never got very cold, but at least it usually kept food safe from the roaches.

She sat on the bed again. The two cots and one three-legged chair were the only furniture. She munched on a pretzel, wishing her father would come. She was going to tell him they had to get out of here, even if it meant asking Uncle Tim to take them in. Uncle Tim, her father's much younger brother, had a dairy farm somewhere in New

Hampshire. She had never seen him, and her father hadn't either since Uncle Tim graduated from college and married a New Hampshire girl whose parents left them the farm. Once every four or five years the brothers exchanged Christmas cards, but that was all.

It was pride that kept her father from getting in touch with his brother. He didn't want to admit he'd lost his big, once-prosperous farm. But Stevie was going to insist. In a place like New Hampshire her father could surely get a farm job. He wasn't trained for the kinds of jobs that were available here. She remembered when her mother was dying of cancer, she had said to Stevie, "Look after your father. He's a good man, but he's not cut out for sorrow and failure. We're farm women; we're strong. Don't ever forget it." She had seen, long before her husband would admit it, that the farm was in trouble: the drought, the government, the new expensive machinery that hadn't been paid for.

Somebody banged on Stevie's door, but it wasn't her father's knock, two short ones, a pause, and another short. She tensed and picked up the bat again. Those doors were not strong. But in a minute whoever it was went away.

She leaned her head back against the wall, trying not to hear the noise outside that never stopped, the car horns, the roar of traffic, the banging of garbage cans, yells, sirens.

She heard the voice of the boy in the next room. She had seen him on the stairs, dragging his little sister along fast, not looking at anybody, as she herself had learned to do. The boy looked about twelve or thirteen, thin and pale with dark hair that needed cutting. The little girl wasn't more than maybe five. She had seen the mother only twice, a pretty young woman with an empty face, too much makeup, flashy clothes. Yesterday she had met a man on the stairs and gone off laughing excitedly, a suitcase in her hand.

Stevie had never spoken to the boy, but she liked to listen to him through the thin wall, especially when he did his pretend radio broadcasts, apparently to amuse his little sister. He did everything from fast-talking ball games to news and weather, in different voices. He was a good mimic. He made Stevie smile and feel somehow comforted, just as his sister probably felt.

"This is Station KILL," the boy's voice said. "Your favorite heavy metal station, and this is your fav-o-rite deejay, Eddie the Deadly."

He had changed his call letters. Yesterday it had been Station HELP. She had wondered about that, but the things he said were funny, so she decided that HELP was a joke. But KILL?

"Here comes the weather report. Listen good. Heavy storm front moving in from the North Pole. Six feet of snow expected tonight. Visibility zero. All traffic halted."

Don't I wish! Stevie thought. It was swelteringly hot in the room.

"Food supplies almost gone," he went on. "Commanding officer deserted. Situation snafu." Something in his voice changed. There was a note of panic. Or was she imagining it? Maybe their mother had really left them.

Or was he just playing a game? She pressed her head closer to the wall, but the "broadcast" had ended without his usual sign-off.

For a few minutes she sat listening, but there were no more sounds. She wondered if the two were all right. Maybe tomorrow she would knock on their door and make sure they were okay. For some reason she felt as if she knew them, perhaps because they were kids like herself, having a hard time.

A little later she tensed at the sound of someone outside her room. She picked up the bat and went toward the door. If she had to hit some druggie, she'd hit him hard.

Her father's secret knock came, and weak with relief she took the chain off and opened the door. Her hands were sweating. "Sometime I'm going to be so scared, I'll forget it's you and hit you with the bat," she said.

"Relax." He came into the room smiling. She hadn't seen him smile in a long time. "We're getting out of this dump. I've got a job."

"Dad! That's wonderful! Where?"

"Alaska."

She gasped. "Alaska!" Then because she knew she sounded dismayed, she said, "Well, it will be clean, anyway."

He gave a sad little laugh. "*I'm* going to Alaska. You're going to your uncle Tim's."

For a few seconds she couldn't speak. "You're going to leave me?"

"Don't sound so tragic. It's just for a while. Till I can get some money saved up. I can't take you to Alaska. This job—a bunch of guys live in a boardinghouse; that's one of the ways I can save money. The pay up there is a lot more than I can make in the lower forty-eight. Cost of living is high, but I'll live as cheap as I can." He loosened his tie. He hated city clothes, but he had tried to look "like something besides an Iowa farm boy," as he said.

"How do you know Uncle Tim will take me?"

"I called him. Somehow when we left the house, I lost his address, but thank God I had his phone number in my wallet. He lives out in the country, got an RFD address, but anyway all you need to know is that he can meet your train tomorrow night at South Station in Boston. I think they tore the station down, but I guess they still call it South. Anyway it's the end of the line. I went to Penn Station and got your ticket. He'll expect you on the train that leaves here just after four. I'll drop you off at the station on my way to the airport."

It was all happening so fast, Stevie was having trouble taking it in. "What if Uncle Tim and his wife don't like me? They don't even know me."

"Why wouldn't they like you?" He sounded impatient. "Look, you've been dying to get out of Manhattan. Here's your chance." He hung his jacket on the back of the chair. He'd had his hair cut.

Stevie was really happy to be getting away from New York, but since her mother's death, her father was all she had. What would she do without him?

"What will you be doing in Alaska?" she said.

"Packing fish." He grinned. "I'll send you a salmon."

The image of her father that she had always had was of

a big man riding a tractor like Ben Hur in his chariot, a serious man taking up the collection at church, the Kiwanis Club vice president, the protective husband and father. Packing fish? She burst into tears.

"There, there, honey." He put his arms around her. "You've been real brave. You haven't cried or complained. You just go ahead and cry it out."

She clung to him and cried for a long time.

Chapter 2

THE NEXT MORNING WHEN SHE AWOKE, SHE LAY still, listening to the city sounds outside, thinking about this being the last day here. What kind of sounds would she wake up to tomorrow? Cows and a rooster crowing, maybe a cat purring, sounds she had grown up with. It would be so good to hear them again. Only what would *they* be like, the unknown uncle and aunt? She knew they had no children. Maybe they didn't like children. She wondered how long her father planned to stay in Alaska.

She wondered if Uncle Tim had a goat. At home, one of the hardest things at the auction was seeing the animals go, especially Elaine, the goat. She loved Elaine.

She sat up abruptly and went into the tiny bathroom to wash and dress. She was homesick enough without lying there bringing on an attack of memories. Someday she would go back. She would never, never live in a city anywhere.

She shivered under the thin trickle of cold water that came out of the shower. She knew there were good things to see in the city, like art museums and theaters, and she wished she could have seen them, but there hadn't been enough money for anything but holding on. Like everyone else here! If she were rich, she'd walk through this hotel and give everybody but the drug pushers a thousand dollars. Two thousand for that nice black woman who lived across the hall, and two for the boy next door.

Maybe she should ask the black woman if she would keep an eye on the boy and his sister. That woman was the only person in the hotel who smiled at her and said hello. She had four little kids and looked as if she would care. Stevie decided to speak to her about the boy.

Her father had gone out, but he had left her a note telling her to pack and be ready to go. He would have to leave her at the station early so he could make his plane.

It didn't take her long to pack. They had left most of their clothes and "personal effects," as the bank called them, in storage, to be sent for when they got settled. They had come to New York by bus.

She packed her clean clothes, her mother's red cashmere pullover, gold bracelet, Parker pen, and her worn copy of Keats's poems with the front page that read, This book belongs to Mary McManus, Grinnell College, 1959. And she packed her own Grinnell sweatshirt that had been her mother's last Christmas present to her. Stevie had planned to go to Grinnell herself, but who knew now?

When she was finished, she went across the hall to the black woman's room and knocked on the door.

The woman took awhile to open the door, and then she didn't take off the chain. "Who is it?"

10

"I'm Stephanie Martin. I live across the hall."

The woman smiled at her, but she looked up and down the corridor before she took the chain off. "Come in." Two small children hung on to her skirt, another was in a high chair, and the oldest peeked out from behind a chair. "You can't be too careful around here," the woman said. "I'm Helen Jean Stafford." She shook hands with Stevie.

Now that she was here, Stevie felt shy about asking Mrs. Stafford what she had come to ask. For a minute she talked to the children, who stared at her with big dark eyes.

"My father and I are leaving today," she said finally.

"Oh, good for you!" Mrs. Stafford said.

"My dad has a job in Alaska, and I'm going to New Hampshire to stay with my uncle. He has a dairy farm."

"Oh, don't that sound wonderful! I'm so glad for you."

"I was wondering if you'd noticed the boy and his sister in the room next to me?"

"Sure have. That no-good mama of theirs looks like gone for good this time. The Lord knows what'll happen to them."

"I was wondering—I mean I guess I was wishing—maybe you could keep them in here at night? So they'd be safe? I saw a guy, I know he was a pusher, trying to talk to the boy down in the lobby the other day. The boy ran away from him. I mean, this is a dangerous place."

The woman made a helpless gesture. "Honey, you are right. But we're packed in here like sardines in a can. I'd take 'em even so, but the welfare'd be down on me like a load of bricks. They'd say I was trying to get extra money or somethin'. Helen Jean, the Welfare Queen." She gave a bitter laugh. "They got us over a barrel. It's the system. I'm takin' my kids back down South just as soon as my mother scrapes together the bus fare for us. I had a job, but it slid right out from under me."

"Oh, I see." Stevie felt so disappointed, she could have cried. She didn't know why those kids were so important to her, but they were. Maybe because she'd had a taste of how awful it would be to get stranded in this place.

"I'll see they get fed," Mrs. Stafford said. "Can't stand to see children go hungry. We don't have much, but we'll share. And I'll speak to my welfare lady about them." She frowned. "Trouble is, they'll separate 'em, first thing. That child takes real good care of his little sister."

"Yes, he does. Well, thank you anyway." She edged toward the door. "What's your name?" she said to the little girl who was nearest to her.

The child stuck her thumb in her mouth. Her mother laughed. "Cat's got her tongue. Tell this nice girl your name, Berta May."

The child took out her thumb and said clearly, "Berta May."

"I hope you have a good time down South." Stevie fumbled with the doorknob. Somehow she always had more trouble getting away from people than getting to see them. She couldn't think of anything smooth and gracious to say, the way her mother would have. "Well," Stevie said again, "thanks anyway."

"Jes' let me check the hall before you go out." Mrs. Stafford looked quickly up and down, then opened the door wide. "You have a beautiful time up there in the country, you hear? And I'll do what I can for those children, though it's precious little I'm good for right now."

They shook hands and wished each other luck again, and Stevie started across the hall. The sound of Mrs. Stafford's door closing and the rattle of the chain as she secured it made Stevie feel depressed. She hesitated, wondering whether to knock on the boy's door. What would she say? Even if they weren't all right, what could she do to help?

She unlocked her own door, but just as she was about to go in, the boy's door opened and he came out, his sister close behind him. He locked his door, put the key in his pocket, and glanced up and down the hall. His glance took in Stevie, but without any recognition. As if, she thought, I'm like the half-dead potted palm by the elevator—no threat, nothing to be paid attention to.

She lingered a moment in her doorway, watching the children walk quickly to the top of the stairs. Suddenly he jumped back and pushed his sister behind him.

A youngish man in tight leather pants and a Michael Jackson shirt ran silently up the stairs in his expensive boat shoes. The boy tried to get back to his room, but the man grabbed him.

"Where you been? I told you to meet me in the lobby an hour ago."

The boy tried to pull away from the man's grip. He looked back nervously at his sister and gestured her away, but she stayed as close as she could. Stevie took her arm, and when the child flinched, she said, "It's all right. Come stand here with me. You'll be safe here." She put her arm around the trembling child and tried to urge her into Stevie's room, but the little girl wasn't about to move far from her brother.

"I told you," the boy said. "I don't want to do it."

The man tightened his grip and put his face close to the boy's. "Listen, friend, when the Duke tells you to show, you show. I got a job for you right now, a rush job, extra bucks. All you gotta do is carry a package six blocks. A hundred bucks for six blocks."

"No," the boy said. His voice shook.

The man started dragging him toward the stairs. "You mean yes, little man. That's what you mean." He had a thin, grayish face. He looked as if he hadn't had enough to eat when he was growing up.

The boy made a lunge to get away. The man hit him across the head. The little girl screamed and tried to run to her brother.

Stevie pushed her inside the room and grabbed the baseball bat that she'd bought to kill rats. The man was standing with his back to her, at the top of the stairs, slightly bent forward as he forced the boy down the steps.

The boy saw her and jerked sideways. She hit the man hard at the bend of his knees. She felt the sickening thunk of the bat on his legs. He screamed and pitched forward on the stairs, grabbing for the railing. He clung to it, moaning.

"Go into my room," Stevie said to the boy, "quick." She was backing toward the door herself. The man on the stairs half turned and pulled a knife from his pocket. He aimed it at Stevie, but he was in an awkward position to throw it. The boy jumped in front of her and shoved her back into her room. She stumbled over the threshold and almost fell. The boy slammed the door shut and attached the chain.

The little girl was crying. Stevie moved her to the other end of the room and sat her down on a bed. "It's all right," she said. "Don't be scared. Your brother's all right now." She noticed for the first time that the boy had a six-inch switchblade in his hand.

"Put that away," she said. "You better not stand by the door. He might have a gun."

"Don't boss me around," the boy snapped. But he folded the knife, put it back in his pocket, and moved away from the door. He looked back at Stevie and shrugged. "Creeps like him get on my nerves."

In spite of the strain of the last few minutes, or perhaps because of it, Stevie laughed. What he had just said seemed like the understatement of all time. The nerve of it made her feel suddenly not only concerned about him, but that she liked him.

The man in the hall was screaming that she had broken his legs. "Do you think I really did?" she said to the boy.

"No such luck." He jerked his head toward the hall, where the man pulling himself painfully up the stairs made a scraping, creaking noise. Then he was pounding on their door.

The boy had his arm around his sister, murmuring comforting things in her ear. She clung to him, shaking and white. He seemed not to be paying attention to the banging on the door, but Stevie noticed the way he took in everything in the room, then looked out the window, checking for a fire escape. He had his knife in his hand again, but he hadn't flicked it open.

Stevie had never seen a switchblade in real life before, only in movies and television. That long, slender blade was terrifying. She wished he didn't have it. On the other hand, that door might splinter if the man outside kept on pounding. She wished somebody would call the cops, but nobody called police in this hotel over anything as ordinary as someone trying to break down a door. She hefted the baseball bat carefully, her heart pounding.

Just then she heard a familiar voice, always welcome but now even more so. Her father was saying, "What do you think you're doing?"

The man's voice changed to a whine. "That kid broke my legs."

"Well, get out of here before I break your neck. Stevie, let me in."

They heard the man limping painfully away. The boy laughed, a small shout of triumph, and hugged his sister. "The Lone Ranger rides again."

Stevie let her father in and relocked the door. He looked at the boy and his sister. "What's going on?"

As briefly as she could, Stevie told him. "That boy saved me from getting a knife thrown at me."

"What's your name, son?" her father said.

"Edward Sanders. This is my sister, Fawn."

"Thanks for your help." Her father shook hands with the boy. Then he turned to Stevie. "Are you packed? I've got to go downstairs and make a couple of phone calls. Will you be all right?"

She nodded.

"Then we'll be taking off, so be ready, okay? I have to make that plane for Valdez." He started to look at his wrist, and she noticed that his watch was gone. So was his onyx ring with the big diamond in the center. "I'll be back in a few minutes." He nodded to the children and left.

"Where you going?" The boy tried to ask it as if it weren't important, but he sounded desolate.

"He's going to Alaska, I'm going to New Hampshire, to my uncle's farm."

"Oh. Well, enjoy. Thanks for hitting the creep."

On an impulse Stevie said, "I'll come in and say good-bye."

"Might as well say it now."

"No, I may want to ask you something." She didn't know really what she was getting at. Just *something* had to be done. If her father gave her some money to take with her, maybe she could give the boy part of it, without telling her father.

Her father had left an envelope on the table. She looked at it after the children had gone to their own room. It was the envelope with the ticket to Boston. Her father had written Uncle Tim's phone number on the envelope. She looked at the ticket to see how much the fare to Boston was. Not a whole lot. Half fare would be less. The boy could pass for under twelve. But what was she thinking about? She couldn't show up in Boston with two extra kids, even if they'd go. She didn't know anything about these kids. Except that Edward was brave and Fawn was frightened, and Mrs. Stafford said they'd been abandoned by their mother. And she liked them.

Maybe welfare people in New Hampshire would be more understanding and let the children stay together in some foster home. Everything here was so—she tried to think of the word her father used with such contempt—so bureaucratic. So heartless. Probably they couldn't help it, with so many to take care of.

Her father came back and gave her her mother's wallet. "There's enough cash in there to tide you over till I get my first paycheck. Then I'll send money to Tim every week. You tell him. I explained, but I don't know if he took it all in, it was such a surprise for him."

She looked in the wallet while her father was in the bathroom. She had to move fast or not move at all. "I'll be right back," she called through the closed bathroom door.

She knocked hard on the children's door. "Edward, open up. It's me, Stevie Martin."

Cautiously he opened the door. "What do you want?"

She went in and closed the door behind her. "I'm going to New Hampshire to stay with my uncle. I want you and Fawn to come with me, okay?"

He stared at her. "Are you out of your mind or what?"

"No. I don't know how we'll work it out when we get there, but it has to be better than this. I have enough money for your tickets. Meet me at Penn Station as soon as you can make it. Is it a big station?"

"Huge." He was still looking at her in disbelief. "This is crazy."

"It's not as crazy as leaving you here. Maybe you can do chores for Uncle Tim. Somehow we'll keep you together. I've got to go. Please come. You'll get killed if you stay here. Where can we meet?"

"Bottom of the stairs into the station, the ones in the middle, where you can see the benches. But I got to think about it."

She heard her father calling her. "I'll be expecting you," she said. "Eddie the Deadly."

His eyes showed surprise. Then he grinned. "Eavesdropper!"

"Radio is public." She ran back to her room. "I'm ready, Dad."

Chapter 3

IT WAS STEVIE'S FIRST RIDE IN A TAXI, AND SHE HOPED it was her last. The friendly, talkative West Indian driver kept one hand on the wheel, turning around to smile at them as he talked. Horns screamed, fenders scraped.

"You won't have too long to wait for your train," her father was saying. "Don't talk to anybody who's not in uniform. An announcer will tell you what track to go to."

She tried to listen to him, but she felt disoriented.

"I wrote Tim's phone number on the ticket envelope. Just don't put that envelope down anyplace and go off without it."

"I won't, Dad. I'll just sit and watch the people."

At the last minute she almost told her father about Edward Sanders and his sister, but the taxi screeched up to the station entrance, and her father was asking the driver to wait while he left his daughter; then they would go to the airport. He had told him twice before, but her father never trusted people with foreign accents to understand what he said.

The driver jumped out and then made a big joke of having unloaded her father's suitcase instead of hers. Meanwhile the cabs behind him honked and the drivers screamed obscenities.

Her father hugged her hard. "You'll be fine. I'll send you my address. Write often."

"I hope Alaska is okay." She didn't want to let go of him.

"I've got to go, honey."

She looked at him and realized that although he hated to leave her, he was excited about going to Alaska. Well, he deserved something good.

She picked up her suitcase and went inside.

The size of the station awed her. Bumping her suitcase along, she went down the long flight of stairs.

People were hurrying in different directions, not looking at each other, heads bent. If you had a movie camera that could speed up the action, it would look like an anthill that had been kicked over. She walked around the station, looking at the newsstands and the shops.

When she got tired of carrying the suitcase, she upended it and sat where she could see the wide staircase just in case Eddie and his sister came. She was quite sure they would not come. She must seem like a crazy stranger to Eddie, asking him to get on a train and go to New Hampshire! She *was* crazy. Suppose they came and Uncle Tim said no way was he going to take in two strange kids even overnight. What would she do then? She must have been out of her mind.

Time went by faster than she expected. She was getting

nervous. What if she went to the wrong track, got on the wrong train? She felt so homesick, she could almost smell the barn at home and hear the cows mooing.

She thought of her mother's favorite Keats poem, "Ode to a Nightingale":

> *the sad heart of Ruth, when, sick for home,*
> *She stood in tears amid the alien corn.*

Tears came to her eyes, thinking of Ruth, so far from home. That had always been her favorite Bible story because it was so touching, but now she understood it in her own heart.

She blinked her tears away impatiently. A person couldn't sit on her suitcase in Penn Station and cry over Ruth, who lived thousands of years ago.

Just then she saw the Sanders children. They came down the long steps hand in hand, looking smaller than she remembered them, Eddie with his shoulders held rigid and his jaw stuck out, not looking left or right, and Fawn hurrying along beside him, bewildered.

Eddie was carrying a big plastic grocery bag. When they reached the foot of the stairs, he glared around the station.

Stevie jumped up, so glad to see them she could have cried out. Never mind if there were problems ahead. At least in that moment she was sure she could handle them. She picked up her suitcase and walked toward them.

Chapter 4

"**W**ELL," EDDIE SAID, "I NEED MY HEAD EXAMINED, but here we are. Anything has to be better than where we were."

He was sitting on the floor with his back to a huge post, Fawn in his lap looking sleepy. Stevie sat on her suitcase.

"You'd better give me the info," Eddie said. "I like to be prepared."

"Well, we had this big farm in Iowa where we grew corn," Stevie began.

"Iowa! I thought Iowa was a joke."

"It's no joke," Stevie said stiffly. "Are you going to listen or not?"

"Sure. I guess it's no funnier than Brooklyn."

As briefly as she could, she told him about her mother's death three years ago, the loss of the farm and her father's desperation, the hope of finding work in New York.

"In New York?" he said. "A guy from a corn farm comes looking for work in *Manhattan*? He'd have a better crack at it on the moon."

"I'm hungry," Fawn said softly.

"In a few minutes, baby." Eddie held her close to him.

Stevie told him about Uncle Tim and how little she knew about him. "For all I know, he may not even show up in Boston. But it seemed as if we'd be better off anywhere than where we were. That drug pusher . . ."

"Yeah, I know. And he wasn't the only one. They pay kids big bucks for running drugs. Just carry a package. I was listenin', I don't mind telling you. Only I figured I'd end up in a trash can with a knife in my back, and then what would happen to Fawn?"

"Your mother really left you, didn't she?"

"She never had us. My mother isn't quite right in the head. Gram said she was shacking up with guys by the time she was in the fifth grade. It was our grandmother brought us up. But she died last month." He said it in a tough voice, but his lip quivered. "It was like *sudden*. She hadn't planned for no heart attack. So the law says our mother is stuck with us. She dumped us in that hotel and took off. That's the whole schmeer. Let's go find something to eat. Our ever-lovin' mother left us five bucks."

They went to a place where Stevie could get them hot dogs, and after they had eaten, Stevie bought their train tickets.

They still had a short time to wait.

"Do the radio," Fawn said. She rummaged in the plastic bag and brought out a Walkman that had no parts, just the outer shell.

"I found it in a trash can," Eddie said. "But honey, Stevie don't want to hear my broadcast."

24

"Yes, I do," Stevie said. "At the hotel I used to listen to you through the wall. You make me laugh."

"All right, here goes." He put the plug in his ear and held the shell of the Walkman in front of his face. He thought for a minute and then began, in a low, fast patter. "You're listening to FM Station WILD, folks, your favorite spot on the dial. News coming up after this word from our sponsor. Stay tuned." He changed to a smooth, oily voice. "Folks, I want to ask you a very personal question. Ladies and gentlemen, how is your love life? Is it drab? Monotonous? Has the glitz gone out of it? My friends, what you need is our brand-new product, Love Me Toothpaste. You'll be the life of the party, the toast of the ball. Friends, Love Me Toothpaste is made from tasty fresh cornflakes mashed up with *glue* and boiled to a fragrant yummy mixture. As you know, most toothpastes are made with paste, but we use glue and that's the secret. At the end we toss in a dash of steak sauce and some ground-up radishes. Friends, it tastes so good, you'll want to eat it! Your teeth will shine like piano keys. So schlep on down to your favorite drugstore and get your Love Me Toothpaste today. Guaranteed to please or your money back. Send me a card, tell me how much you love it. And now back to Jeremiah for the news. Stay tuned."

Fawn was rocking with giggles. A well-dressed woman with a briefcase smiled at them as she went by.

"Eddie, where did you learn to do that?" Stevie said.

"Me and Gram worked up an act. We did soap operas and mysteries and game shows and all kinds of commercials. I'd do Phil Donahue and Gram would do Oprah."

"Your grandmother sounds like fun."

"She was." He looked sad for a moment, and Stevie wished she hadn't brought it up. Then he shrugged. "Well, it's the breaks. When you get old, you die, whether you're nice or not." He jumped up to look at the clock again. "Why don't they post those train gates?"

They moved toward the track area.

"Look," Stevie said. "There's the gate number." She pointed to the sign that had just given the track number for the train to Boston. They joined the jostling, pushing crowd, Eddie carrying Stevie's suitcase and holding tight to Fawn's hand, Stevie clutching Eddie's plastic bag in one hand and the ticket envelope and four candy bars in the other. The candy was beginning to melt, and as soon as she could make enough space around her, she shoved the envelope into her jacket pocket to keep it from getting smeared with chocolate. She should have put those dumb candy bars in Eddie's bag, she thought, feeling how squishy they were getting. She held her hand in front of her, hoping she wasn't getting chocolate all over the people next to her. She hated being jostled. One man shoved hard against her, and then was gone without even saying excuse me.

But finally they reached the bottom of the stairs, and Eddie pointed to the right train. He and Fawn led the way. Stevie felt relieved to get out of that crush of people.

Eddie asked a brakeman which car they should board, and the man pointed to a car up near the engine.

They hauled their baggage into the car, and Eddie chose two seats at the end of the car so they could sit facing each other. Eddie was efficient, Stevie thought; you'd think he'd been traveling all his life.

He and Fawn sat on the seat facing backward, and Stevie settled into the other one.

"Well," Eddie said, "we're off to see the wizard."

Chapter 5

EDDIE LOOKED DOWN AT FAWN. SHE LOOKED TIRED.
"A train," he said. "Not a subway but a real train. Like
it?"

She smiled. "I like it. Does it go?"

"It'll go in a minute. Fast." He'd never been on a train
himself. It was exciting, but he felt very uneasy about
where they were going. He didn't even know this farm
kid with the broad shoulders and the corn-colored hair.
Maybe she was some kind of nut. Here they were, on a
train, heading for Boston, to be met by an uncle she didn't
even know, who didn't expect two extra kids. Was that
weird or what?

The train gave a jerk, and Fawn looked at him with
alarm.

"It's okay." It seemed as though she was younger somehow since Gram died and they'd had that shocker of a week
with their goofy mother. Fawn clung to him all the time.
It made him nervous, but he didn't want her to feel scared.

The train was pulling out of the station. A tall young black man in a business suit came on at the last minute and sat in the seat behind them. Eddie wondered if he were a stockbroker. Men in suits like that always looked to him as if they worked on Wall Street. The man caught his eye and gave him a friendly smile.

Stevie was spreading the half-melted candy bars on a Kleenex on the seat beside her and wiping her hands. Eddie grinned. It reminded him of Gram always telling him to wash his hands.

Stevie put her hand in her jacket pocket and rummaged around for a moment, the expression on her face changing.

"What's the matter?" he said.

She went through all her pockets, looking more and more frantic.

"Is something the matter, Eddie?" Fawn said in the voice that sounded anxious so often lately.

"Nothing, baby. Hey, look at that woman's purple hat." He pointed toward a woman on the platform as the train slid by. "Isn't that the purplest hat you ever saw?"

"I've seen purpler."

"Eddie," Stevie said. "Somebody stole our tickets."

"What!" He thought she was kidding. He *hoped* she was kidding.

"I put the envelope in my pocket. It couldn't have fallen out. These pockets are really deep." She stood up and went through her pockets again. She stood out in the aisle, looking all around the seat.

"Something wrong, miss?" the black man said.

"Our tickets. I had them in the envelope in my pocket. They couldn't have fallen out."

"Oh-oh. Did the envelope show?"

"Yes, I guess it did. I had my hands full of candy that was melting, so when we started for the train I shoved the envelope into my pocket." A thought occurred to her. "A man in that crowd bumped against me really hard and then took off. He didn't even say he was sorry. Maybe he took them."

"They'll throw us off the train," Eddie said. As Fawn tugged at his sleeve, he said, "Don't, Fawn. I got to think. We'll fix it. Don't I always fix it?"

She nodded and relaxed, leaning her head against his arm.

"Maybe I can explain to the conductor." Stevie was sitting down again. "My uncle could pay him on the other end."

Eddie didn't believe that for a minute. He had never seen much generosity from public officials, especially toward kids. The conductor would think they were trying to hook a free ride. He wished he had washed his shorts and shirt last night so he wouldn't look like a street kid. Fawn looked okay. She always did. And Stevie in her jeans and white shirt and denim jacket looked as if she had never been dirty in her life.

She was looking at the money in her wallet, counting it.

"I got five dollars," he said.

"If he won't let us ride to Boston, we'll just go as far

as we've got enough money for. Maybe it will be close enough so I can phone my uncle—" She stopped and clapped her hand to her mouth. "His phone number was on that envelope. I don't have it."

"So look him up in the phone book, ask Information, whatever."

She swallowed. "I don't know where he lives."

"All you need is the town."

"He doesn't live in a town. He's got a farm out in the country. It's an RFD address or something."

Eddie frowned, trying to think. "You could page him at South Station."

"They've torn down the station."

He groaned. It was worse than frustrating; it was desperate. But then he looked at Stevie's stricken face and knew he'd better pull himself together. He could see how bad she felt, screwing everything up not only for herself but for Fawn and him. A city kid would have had more sense than to put something valuable in her pocket, but Stevie didn't know. And she had guts. He remembered the sound of her baseball bat hitting that drug creep in the knees.

The door to the car opened with a pneumatic wheeze, letting in a blast of hot, smoggy air. Eddie took one look at the conductor and knew that this guy was not going to go for any sad songs. He looked like a man who hated his job.

The conductor went on down the aisle, balancing himself with his hands on the backs of the seats. He wasn't picking up tickets yet.

The black man behind them said softly, "Good luck."

"Thank you," Stevie said. Her voice sounded small. She had counted out the bills in her wallet, put one back, and folded the others. She kept her eyes on the aisle, watching for the conductor. Then she took a deep breath, as if she were taking hold of herself.

"Where did you and your grandmother live?" she said, trying hard to sound normal.

"Brooklyn."

"Is that like Manhattan?"

"Nah. It's a real place. Historic. We lived on the top floor of a brownstone."

"What happened to all your grandmother's things?"

"My mother pawned what she could and gave the rest to the Good Will."

"Ours is in storage," Stevie said. "I don't know if we'll ever get it out."

"The only thing I got to keep," Eddie said, "was the mezuzah that Gram hung on her door. She hadn't gone to the synagogue since she married Gramps—he was Irish." He nodded toward the plastic bag. "It's in the bottom." He had wrapped it carefully in one of his clean T-shirts and then covered it with his and Fawn's clean undershorts, T-shirts, shorts, socks, and toothbrushes. It wasn't a whole lot to start a new life with.

He saw Stevie stiffen, and he looked back to see the conductor coming up the aisle toward them, picking up tickets.

"Look cool," Eddie said. "Look like you had tickets

clear to Europe and a Mercedes waiting for you at the other end, but some creep robbed you. Look like you got a filthy rich uncle waiting in Boston." He reached over and touched her arm. "Relax. There isn't any bomb under your seat."

She gave him a shaky smile. "What'll I say?"

"Tell him the truth. If you act antsy, he's saying to himself 'She's lying.' " He'd think that anyway, but there was no sense saying so and making her more jumpy. If anybody had ever told him he'd be riding illegal on a train to Boston with a kid from a corn farm, he'd have laughed himself silly.

"Tickets, tickets." The conductor's growly voice was louder as he worked his way toward them.

Stevie was sitting stiffly upright, her dark blue eyes wide. She clutched the roll of bills in her hand inside her pocket, out of sight.

He stood beside them, a dumpy man with a permanent scowl. "Tickets," he said impatiently.

Stevie cleared her throat. "I had our tickets in my pocket. When I got on the train, they were gone. Somebody must have taken them."

The conductor gave her a long, hard look. She blinked, but she didn't look away. "My uncle is meeting us in Boston. He'll pay you." In a voice fainter still, she said, "If you would be so kind."

"You'll have to get off at the first stop. We don't carry freeloaders. Get off at New Rochelle, and don't try any tricks like this again."

The black man leaned forward. "She's telling you the truth, conductor. She was hunting all around here looking for her tickets. Couldn't you let them ride to Boston?"

The conductor gave him a cold look. "This isn't the Welfare Express. *You* got a ticket?"

The man handed him his ticket, shaking his head.

"Conductor," Stevie said, "sir, how far could we go on this much money?" She handed him the wad of bills.

Annoyed at the delay, the conductor flipped through the bills. "This'll take you about one third of the way, if you've got another three dollars."

Quickly the black man reached in his pocket and handed the conductor three bills.

Grumbling, the conductor pocketed the money and punched out tickets for them. Then he bustled on to the next car.

"Thank you very much," Stevie said to the black man. "I can pay you, though. I kept back a little."

He shook his head. "My pleasure. You don't want to get dumped in New Rochelle. The cops'd pick you up first thing. Farther away, you'll get along better. I wish I had enough bucks to get you to Boston."

"You're very, very nice, " Stevie said.

Eddie nodded at him. "Thanks a lot, mister." That was a good guy.

He looked at Stevie's worried face. "Take it cool. Sometimes it rains and sometimes it pours, but it don't hardly ever drown you." He put his arm around Fawn, who had fallen asleep.

Chapter 6

THE TRAIN WAS SLOWING DOWN. STEVIE STOOD UP AND lifted the suitcase from the rack. She felt as if she were in shock. What were they going to do when they got dumped off at some station in Connecticut? She'd got these kids into this terrible mess, and she didn't know how to handle it.

Maybe the best thing would be to find the police station. She wanted to tell Eddie how sorry she was. He was being such a good sport about it.

She stooped down and looked out the window. Just an ordinary city.

Eddie was waking Fawn. "We're going to get off here, kiddo."

"Are we there?" Fawn asked sleepily.

"Well, we're somewhere."

The train jolted to a stop, and the conductor threw open the door, beckoning to them. Eddie grabbed the suitcase and Fawn's hand and went out first. Stevie followed, carrying the Sanderses' bag. As she went by the man who had tried to help, he reached for her hand and put some-thing in it, a piece of paper folded small.

"Call your mama," he said.

"Thank you. You've been nice." She was so touched by his kindness, her eyes filled with tears.

"Good luck, and take it easy."

"Hurry it up." The conductor was scowling at her. "Haven't got all night." He reached out to help her down the iron steps, but she ignored his hand.

A man got off, went to a parked car, and drove away. The station was closed. The conductor swung onto the steps and waved his arm at the engineer, and the train began to move.

The children stood there watching the cars glide past them.

"May you fall into a barrel of molasses headfirst," Eddie called after the conductor, who had already disappeared.

"Why?" Fawn said. "Was he a bad man?"

"Mean," Eddie said. "Mean as a snake."

"I'm hungry," Fawn said.

Stevie opened her hand to look at what the man had given her. "A twenty! That man gave me a twenty-dollar bill, the man behind us."

"Wow!" Eddie said. "We live again!"

"I still have some of my father's money left," she said, "so we wouldn't have starved—yet—but now we can save that. What a nice guy!"

"May he *never* fall into a barrel of molasses," Eddie said. "There's a little greasy spoon across the road. You want I should get some burgers?"

"Couldn't we all go?"

He looked at the suitcase. "Three kids prowling around town carrying a suitcase and a big plastic bag might as well hang a sign around our necks that says 'Runaways.' We'd have the cops on our back right off."

"Shouldn't we go to the police anyway? Maybe they could help."

"No way," Eddie said firmly. "Not me. You can go if you want, but not Fawn and me. We get into the clutches of Welfare, and right away they separate us and put us in foster homes." He took hold of Fawn's hand. "No way."

Stevie suddenly felt so tired, she wanted to fall down in a heap and never get up. "All right, we'll stay here."

"Are you going to leave me?" Fawn sounded frightened.

"I'm just going over there to get us some food." He turned her around and pointed out the restaurant. "You and Stevie get to guard the bags. I'll be right back, honest."

It was a typical down-by-the-tracks section, with a run-down café, a shoe repair shop, a two-story warehouse, and stores with false fronts, all of them needing paint. The restaurant had a faded sign that said Depot Square Lunch, and a Budweiser sign flashed in the window.

"See, they serve beer in there," he said to Fawn, who was still looking worried. "I can't take you into a bar. Gram wouldn't like me doing that."

"All right," she said.

"So—burgers for everybody? With mustard, relish, onions, tomatoes, apples and oranges, red roses, hold the marshmallows?" He had made Fawn laugh, so she would be all right now. "Be right back." He took the twenty and walked around the small station, taking it in as he went. If he could pry open one of those windows, they could sleep safe in there, but he didn't know when the station was open. Someone might find them. They'd have to find someplace, though. The sky looked like more rain.

He needed to talk to Gram. It was a habit he couldn't do without, so he made up the conversations in his head.

Closed-circuit station EDDX3 to GRAM7, do you read me?

GRAM7 to EDDX3, I read you loud and clear.

Live broadcast. Subject now crossing road in search of provisions for troops. Whoops! Almost ran into gentleman in derby hat riding bicycle. Got called filthy name.

How many times I gotta tell you, don't jaywalk.

No other way but flying, and subject's got no pilot's license. Subject now stopping to case the joint. Cruising around parking lot. Two trucks: Bondi's Fresh Vegetables, Mayflower Movers; one semi; one Honda four-door, dented fender, New Jersey plates; one camper, New York plates.

Never mind that. Go get the sandwiches. Pastrami for Fawn.

Walking around camper. Rear door unlocked.

I'm telling you once, I'm telling you twice, get out of there.

Subject gets in. Nice and cool. Trips over six-pack. Sits down. Dark in here. If subject falls asleep and wakes up in New York, could he help it?

He could help it. Move!

Back in the old neighborhood, subject could live on the street, join up with the B8 Bombers, hang out with them.

They beat you up last year.

Howie would speak up for me. You always liked Howie. Till he went wrong.

He went wrong. He's a hood, a pusher, who knows. He's not even Jewish. Eddie, schlep into that deli and do what you came for. I mean it.

Reception's not too good in here. I don't read you.

You're reading me like a book. Get out of that van.

Not van—camper. Oops! Owner approaching, whistling "Stardust." Must be an old guy. He won't be tough to handle.

You've got the twenty. What is Fawn going to eat—coal dust?

Diesel, Gram. Trains haven't used coal for years. Door slamming, engine starting now, vroom vroom! Starting to roll . . .

EDWARD! What are you doing to me?

Eddie jumped out of the camper and ducked behind the Honda. The camper door slammed shut and opened again as the man drove over a pothole. He braked, jumped out, latched the door, then drove away.

Eddie was sweating.

EDDX3 to GRAM7, you read me?

Roger.

It was the devil telling me to hop the camper. That's what Gramps would say.

Devil shmevel. The only devil you got is in your own skull. Go get those sandwiches. Over and out already.

Eddie sauntered into the café trying to look casual. Not many people were there. The old couple who must belong to the Honda were eating pot roast and fried potatoes in one of the booths. Truck drivers at the end of the bar were drinking beer and watching baseball on the big TV. The young waitress leaned on the cash register looking bored.

"What's your pleasure, friend?" she said.

Eddie put the twenty where she could see it, glanced at the menu, and did some rapid arithmetic. "Three super burgers with everything, a big order of fries, and three chocolate milk shakes."

She slapped the burgers on the grill and began to make the shakes. "You going to eat all that by yourself?" She glanced out the window.

"No way. My family's up the street, getting gas."

She nodded, not really curious. She threw some sliced fries into the fryer.

He looked at the TV. He wasn't too interested if it wasn't the Mets. Just to make conversation he said, "Who's playing?"

"Who knows?" she said. "Who cares?"

"You don't like baseball?" He was shocked. It seemed un-American not to like baseball.

"I hate baseball." She flipped the burgers and turned the fries. "I hate hamburgers." She leaned on the counter and lowered her voice. "I hate truck drivers."

"Lady, you need another job."

She laughed. "What an idea man. They could use you on Madison Avenue. I'll tell you a secret; I'm learning to run a computer. I'm going to be a hacker and put all the big companies out of business. Maybe the government too."

He grinned. This was an okay woman.

One of the truckers growled at her without turning away from the TV. "Where's the Bud, Marie? Keep 'em comin', will ya?"

She got the beer cans and mimed throwing one of them at the trucker's head. Then she slid them along the counter. "Comin' at you, Jake."

The men reached back and got them without taking their eyes off the game. She put the hot fried potatoes into a carton and expertly poured the shakes into tall cups. "Where you from?"

"Brooklyn." It looked to Eddie as if she had given him about one and a half shakes in each cup.

"Well, Brooklyn this is not. Are you going or coming?"

"That's a good question," Eddie said.

This time she laughed so heartily, the Honda couple looked up from their pot roast and smiled vaguely. She finished the burgers, put all the individual bags into one big bag, and took his twenty. "You're a funny kid," she said. "That's my first laugh today."

When she gave him his change, he put a one-dollar bill flat on the counter. "I hope you get to be a champion hacker."

She looked at the dollar and then at him, her face softening. "What's your name?"

"Eddie."

"Eddie," she said, "I'll remember you."

As Eddie started across the road, he heard Fawn scream.

Chapter 7

EDDIE RACED ACROSS THE ROAD, CLUTCHING THE BIG bag of food against his chest. Fawn had sounded terrified, and his heart was pounding against his ribs. He shouldn't have left her there; anything could happen.

He tore around the corner of the station and saw Stevie chasing what looked like a hobo. She was waving her baseball bat and yelling. Fawn cowered against the side of the station, beside Stevie's suitcase, which was open and partly unpacked.

He dropped the bag of food on the wide stone step and said, "What happened?" Stevie seemed to have the situation in hand, so he pulled Fawn into his arms. She was shaking.

"He grabbed me," she said. "That dirty man grabbed me."

"It's all right now, honey. He's gone." He watched the man run across the tracks, over the wire fencing, and out of sight.

Breathing hard, Stevie walked back.

"It's all right, Fawn," she said. "He's gone."

"He might come back," Fawn said.

"Not while Wonder Woman is here," Eddie said. "That Stevie is a one-woman army."

"Look, Eddie brought us some food. Doesn't it smell terrific?" Stevie put her arm around Fawn.

Eddie looked at Stevie, his eyebrows raised in a question.

"Just a railroad bum," she said. "He snuck up on us before we saw him. I was trying to sort out what I could take with me and what to leave behind. Fawn saw him first and yelled, and he grabbed her."

Eddie sat down with Fawn on his knees. He gazed at Stevie with renewed admiration. "You're pretty handy with that bat."

"It was wedged in the suitcase crosswise, and for a minute I didn't think I could get it loose. When it came out, it came with such a whoosh, it hit him in the head." She laughed. "He was stooping over to see what he could steal, and all he got was a wallop on the head." She waved off Eddie's admiration. "Oh, he's not the first bum I've chased off. They used to try to steal our chickens."

"Maybe they're hungry," Fawn said.

"Well, I am, anyway." Eddie opened up the bags and gave the big one to Stevie. "Maybe you can use that to carry things in. It'll look like you're carrying food instead of the family jewels." He was looking at the small leather case with Stevie's mother's monogram in the corner.

While they ate, she explained about the leather case. "It's about all I have of my mother's."

He told her more about Gram's mezuzah. "It's twenty-two lines from the Bible on parchment rolled in a wooden tube."

When they had eaten every bite, Eddie found a trash can, while Stevie folded up the things she could get into the paper bag: the leather case fitted in the bottom, and on top she put two T-shirts, underwear, socks, toothbrush, soap, a cotton sweater, and her mother's red cashmere. She held up her Grinnell sweatshirt. "How about wearing it?" she said to Eddie. "Maybe it's cool enough now. It's going to rain."

He tied the sleeves around his waist. "What's Grinnell?"

"It's the college I was going to."

"Come on, am I wearing a girls'-school shirt?"

"No, it's coed, and don't go macho on us. Fawn, do you want to wear my blue cardigan? We can push up the sleeves."

The sweater hung down below Fawn's knees, but she only giggled.

"You can carry it if it gets too hot."

There was nothing to do but throw the suitcase and the things left into the trash can. Stevie felt like crying. They'd taken so many vacations with that suitcase.

"Well," Eddie said, "let's hit the road. Walk easy, like locals." He took Fawn's hand, and they walked across the road.

The sky was darker than usual at this hour, with gray clouds piling up.

"So Stevie is our sister, all right? And we're on our way home for supper," Eddie said to Fawn. "Just pretend."

He looked up at the sky. "Let's move it. We don't want to get wet."

They passed stores that were still open: a Radio Shack, a supermarket, a drugstore, a Burger King doing a brisk business. The hardware store was closed, and the office supply store, and Jeannette's Shoppe, Regular and Large Sizes. A few cars went by, but there was no one on the sidewalks except a group of teenagers, two boys on bikes and three girls, laughing and chattering in front of the drugstore. No one paid any attention to them.

Eddie glanced up the side streets, residential streets with small, neat houses on small lots with well-mown lawns.

He and Stevie exchanged glances as they passed the white, steepled Methodist church.

"File it away as a maybe," he said, "if nothing better turns up."

Fawn was jumping cracks in the sidewalk. "Where are we going?"

"Looking for a nice place to spend the night. It's going to rain, and we don't want to get wet, right?"

Three blocks further on he paused to look up a dirt road where there was only one old house on the right, set back from the street behind a tall hedge; and farther along, on the other side of the street a big, faded brick school building, three stories high, square and ugly.

"Who wants to go to school?" Eddie said.

"Hey!" Stevie said. "Do you think we could get in? Maybe they have summer school, though, like at night."

"Let's take a look."

"It would be perfect."

"Stay cool," Eddie said, as Stevie began to walk faster. "We're local kids stopping to throw a ball around the playground. Or something. Or taking a shortcut. Don't look so happy, Stevie."

She laughed. Fawn laughed, too, just because Stevie and Eddie seemed more cheerful.

They cut across a field to the back of the school, where there was a volleyball court, and beyond it a baseball diamond. Eddie put his paper bag on the wide granite steps and began to hit a punching bag that hung from a metal pole. Stevie put her bag down, too, and she and Fawn sat on the steps.

"There might be a watchman," Eddie said. "Stevie, you sort of prowl around the building and case the joint, all right? Fawn, you guard the bags."

Stevie wandered around the building, trying to look as if she were not doing anything in particular. She noticed the locked doors, the windows too high to reach. Making sure she wasn't being watched, she tried a fire door, but it didn't move.

In the front a temporary sign read Summer Classes Begin June 28. Register Now!

When she came around to the other side, she discovered windows at ground level, covered with wire netting. She bent down to look in. When her eyes adjusted to the dim light inside, she saw the gym with a basketball court and a bank of bleachers. It would be perfect if they could just get in! There'd be shower rooms and toilets and mats they could sleep on. But how to get in?

One window had a square area cut in the ground, cemented on the sides with a drain at the bottom. She let herself down into it. It was about waist high. She tried to loosen the wire on the window, but it didn't give.

While she was peering inside, trying to will the place to let them in, Eddie and Fawn came running around the corner of the building.

"Perfect," he said. He lowered Fawn into the space beside Stevie. "Keep down. Somebody just drove up in the back, looks like a janitor."

"Did he see you?"

"No. Keep out of sight. I'll check out the scene. Don't, repeat, *do not* move out of there till I come. Got it?"

"Got it." She watched him run along close to the wall. She sat down on the drain, cramping her legs up under her, and pulled Fawn down beside her.

"Where's Eddie going?" Fawn was getting anxious.

"Nowhere. He's right back there at the corner. Don't worry, he'll be back in a minute." She wondered why she had so much faith in that boy. Sometimes she resented take-charge people, especially boys and especially when they weren't even as old as she was, but she trusted Eddie. There had been a minute back there at the restaurant when he was gone so long with the twenty dollars that it had crossed her mind that he might leave Fawn with her and take off for New York. But seconds later she had known for sure that he would not.

With alarming suddenness the lights went on in the gym. Stevie shrank as far away from the window as she could get. She wished her legs weren't so long.

"It's squashy in here," Fawn said.

"It won't be long. Just keep very still, like a mouse."

Fawn tilted her head on one side and squinted her eyes. "I'm a mouse, and that big cat in there doesn't even know I'm here."

"That big cat" was a man in white overalls going over the gym floor with a wide mop. He picked up some litter and put it in a big trash can. After a while, when he had finished mopping, he disappeared with the trash can, and Stevie heard the opening of a heavy door. It sounded like the metal door where they had been sitting, at the back. Now she could hear him whistling a Tracy Chapman song and not getting it right. You couldn't really whistle Tracy Chapman. She wanted to giggle, thinking how surprised he would be if she started whistling with him. She wondered where Eddie was.

She heard the clatter and crash of a dumpster, then a few minutes later the clang of the big door closing again. It probably locked automatically from the inside. Her grade school, which she had to graduate from "in absentia," as the letter from the principal said, had one of those pneumatic metal things so you could close the door slowly, not slam it. For just a second she wanted so badly to be back in that school, she felt weak.

The lights in the gym went out. Fawn tried to stretch her legs, but there wasn't room. "Can I stand up?" she said.

"Wait just a minute longer, if you can," Stevie said.

"Where's Eddie?"

"Coming in a minute." But she was beginning to worry.

48

Where was he? Could the janitor have discovered him? You wouldn't put a kid in jail or anything just because he was hanging around a school, would you? Unless he'd gone inside, and the man called it breaking and entering?

She heard the sound of a car starting up and driving off, and it took all her self-control not to jump out of the enclosure to look. Eddie, she said silently, be all right. Don't be in that man's car! The feeling of being trapped in the cement square filled her with panic.

Then there he was, running silently along the building. "Follow me, quick." He lifted Fawn out and gave a hand to Stevie. "Stay right behind me."

Her legs were so numb, she almost fell down. She stumbled along behind him, staying in the darkness cast by the building. Stabs of pain shot up her legs, and her feet felt frozen.

He led them to the back door, which was propped open by a rock. There he hustled them inside, threw away the rock, and let the door close, bracing it so it wouldn't slam.

"Whew!" he said. "I was scared the rock would slip out."

"I can't believe it," Stevie said. "I can't believe we're inside."

"Why is it so dark?" Fawn said.

"You'll get used to it in a minute," Eddie said. "We can't put on the lights because we don't want anyone to know we're here."

"The big cat," Fawn said, understanding.

As their eyes grew used to the dimness, Stevie saw that they were in a corridor that led to a flight of stairs, and through a door in front of them was the gym. No gym had ever looked so beautiful to her before. "How did you manage it?"

"When he went to the dumpster, I snuck in and hid. After he left, I braced the door open while I came to get you. Pretty neat, huh? Our own Waldorf-Astoria."

"It's perfect. Do you think he'll come back?" She heard the rain starting, a soft patter on the side of the building.

"Yeah. He talks to himself. He had to do some painting, and he was mad because he forgot the rollers."

"There must be phones upstairs. I could start trying to find Uncle Tim."

"Maybe real early in the morning. The guy's coming right back, and tomorrow there might be somebody in the office if they're registering for summer school."

"I have to go to the bathroom," Fawn said.

Eddie showed her where the girls' room was. "When you wash your hands, try not to splash. The janitor would notice."

Later they heard him come back, and they huddled in the dark while he worked upstairs, whistling, for about an hour. Finally he left.

"Station WHERE," Eddie said, holding an imaginary mike. "This is your old Storyteller, Uncle Sandy. You've just heard the perils and problems of our three heroic little children, Steverion, Feathered Fawn, and Outrageous Eduardo. As usual, they've triumphed over Evil, Bad Luck, and a Vicious Jackass. Pleasant dreams, little children everywhere. And now for a shot of rhythm and blues. Stay tuned for the Mad Maestro of Metal."

50

Chapter 8

STEVIE AND FAWN SLEPT ON MATS IN THE EQUIPMENT room and Eddie moved a mat to a corner near the end of the short hallway, where he could see any lights that showed up in the parking lot.

He slept lightly, waking whenever he heard the slightest noise. Once he thought he heard a car, and he sat up so quickly, he cracked his head on the drinking fountain, but the car went on down the road.

It began to rain hard after midnight, and when they woke in the morning, it was pouring. Stevie and Eddie had a conference and decided to stay where they were till the weather cleared.

Stevie found the cafeteria on the same floor as the gym. The cupboards were empty except for a large box of graham crackers and two institutional-size cans of peaches. She brought them back, with plastic spoons, and they had breakfast.

Eddie got one of the basketballs from the supply room, and he and Stevie played a two-man game, doing lay-ups and foul shots and figuring out a point system for themselves. Fawn watched them for a while and then unearthed a checkerboard from the supply room.

Stevie left Eddie teaching Fawn how to play checkers, while she went cautiously upstairs to look for a phone.

It made Eddie nervous to have her upstairs. With the rain making such a racket, it would be hard to hear a car. He wished he were as sure as she was that she would find her uncle and everything would turn out great. He ought to make some kind of plan, because even if she did find him, this uncle was not going to jump with joy over taking in two scruffy-looking kids who talked like Brooklyn and looked like Brooklyn. Probably the guy was anti-Semitic, and, in spite of his Irish grandfather and his God-alone-knew-what kind of father, Eddie knew he looked Jewish. He looked like Gram, and he was proud of it, but that wouldn't cut any ice with some mean, bigoted Yankee farmer. As soon as he saw a chance for Fawn and him to make a break, they'd better do it.

They'd have to depend on those soup kitchens churches were supposed to have, or on the Salvation Army. The trouble with that was, they'd attract attention. People would ask questions. If only he were taller. In this country you had to be tall to get any respect. Well, they'd have to play it by ear. Sooner or later he was sure he could get a job, errand boy or something. Maybe he could even work on a farm, although he didn't know which end of a cow was up.

He showed Fawn how to make a move that would take three of his men out of the game. She was a smart little kid, and if he looked Jewish, she looked like some blond princess out of those fairy tales Gram used to read them. Whoever Fawn's father was, he must have been a good-looking Anglo.

"Move this one over here." He showed her. "I think you're going to beat me." He wished Stevie would come back. Maybe the school people were too lazy to come out in the rain. He wished he hadn't promised Gram he'd never steal anything. He'd be a real good shoplifter.

Stevie appeared so silently that Eddie jumped and knocked off some of the checkers.

Angry at himself for having been unwatchful, he said, "Where've you been all this time?"

"Well, I haven't been up there enjoying the scenery." She sat down on the bench. "How's the game going?"

"See if you can beat her." He picked up the fallen checkers and arranged them on the board. "You have any luck with the phone?"

"No." She seemed discouraged.

After Stevie and Fawn started playing, Eddie got the old Walkman. Better cheer up Stevie somehow. "Greetings, friends," he said into the shell of the radio. "This is your old buddy Eddie the Unlikely coming at you from your favorite spot on the dial, Station KOZY. And you know what those call letters spell, friends—they spell ENTERTAINMENT. We've got a fine sunny day outside here, but in the studio the atmosphere is electric, I mean *eee*-lectric, as the two checkers champions battle it out for the world champeenship. On our left is Furious Fawn, Featherweight Champ of Brooklyn N'Yawk, and on our right is Stupendous Stephanie, Miracle Mover of Ioway. Yes-siree, folks, we got a match here that'll stand you on your head. As I'm watching, Furious Fawn moves her red in a spectacular leap over Stupendous Stephanie's black, and she's going to—yes, folks, she's going to eliminate another black and—she's done it! Furious Fawn is rolling toward victory. She's jumping, she's moving, she's leapfrogging. Ladeez and Gents, she has just won game and match. Furious Fawn of Brooklyn N'Yawk is the new champeen of the century. What a game, folks. In all my years of broadcasting, I have *never*. . . Over to you for the hog prices, Henry. Folks, this is KOZY. Stay tuned." He flopped on his back on the bleacher bench. Fawn was giggling, Stevie was smiling. Mission accomplished. And oh, man, he was tired. He wished he could clear out, go it alone, hitch rides, hop freights, worry about nobody.

Chapter 9

EDDIE AND FAWN WERE ASLEEP IN THE GYM. IT WAS Stevie's turn to keep watch. As far as she could tell, it was about eight o'clock. In the dusky dark of the gym it was hard to read the big wall clock.

The rain had finally stopped. She walked up to the front entrance to the gym, where a broad flight of stairs led to the main hall of the school. Being in a school when it was absolutely silent was a weird experience. You expected lots of noise and activity. She could hear the slapping sounds of her sneakers on the wooden floor.

In the morning they would have to make a move, even if it rained again. For one thing, they were out of food. She hoped she would never see a canned peach again as long as she lived.

She had never hitched a ride, and she couldn't imagine any truck driver or anyone else stopping to pick up three kids, but maybe if she went back to the Burger King and found somebody safe-looking, like a middle-aged couple with New Hampshire or even Massachusetts plates, she could get up her nerve to ask for a ride. She and Eddie would have to think up a reasonable story.

She thought about her father. Pretty soon he would find out that she had never arrived in Boston, and he would be worried to death. She wondered if she could call the mayor of Valdez and ask for the address of the fish-packing place. Maybe there were a dozen of them. It might not even be in Valdez; that might just be where his plane came in. She could write the Chamber of Commerce and ask them to find her father. Only how would *he* find *her* when she didn't know where she was going? Her head ached. She sat down on one of the benches and closed her eyes.

Suddenly the lights in the gym blazed. For a moment Stevie was too startled to move. Then she shot out of the gym and ran to Eddie. He was already on his feet. They slid along the corridor, backs to the wall, and went into the supply room, where Fawn was sitting up. There was no light in the supply room, but sounds upstairs had awakened her.

They sat huddled together, praying that the janitor wouldn't decide to clean up the supply room. Time went by. Maybe he wasn't even coming downstairs; maybe all the lights in the building went on at once.

Stevie got up and opened the door a crack, just enough to see out into the gym. It was empty, but as she started to turn away, a young man in blue jeans and a T-shirt came running down the backstairs, passing so close to her, she thought he would surely see her. But he kept going and went into the boys' locker room.

The janitor came down the front stairs. "Hey, Alex, you find what you want?"

"Yeah, I will, and I owe you ten bucks, remember?" The boy, who looked about seventeen or eighteen, came out and handed the janitor a bill. He was tall, Stevie noticed, and quite handsome, with short curly black hair and dark eyes. He had one of those strong noses that looked like the Roman and Greek statues in her mother's picture book of the Louvre Museum.

"You didn't call me up in the shank of the evening just for that. I trust you. And you didn't have to meet me here. What's up?" The janitor sat down beside him on a bench.

"I'm leaving town. My old man just threw me out of the house." He showed him a bruise on his cheekbone. "See? For real. I'm splitting this burg."

"Oh, that Joe and his temper. What'd you do to make him so mad?"

"I told him I turned down my scholarship to Dartmouth."

"Why'd you do that?"

"Because I don't want to go to college. I'm a Vo-Tech kind of guy."

"Like that cabinetmaker you were helping out?"

"Right. He doesn't need me this summer, but somebody will. I can do that stuff."

"You'll never make a million with a hammer and a chisel."

"You sound like my old man."

"Well, kids and parents. It's the way it goes."

"It went fine with his other three kids. That ought to be enough. He's got their diplomas framed in silver on his office wall. You can't get in or out of Joe Caras's office without hearing how he came to this country just an ignorant Greek boy and now he owns three supermarkets and he's got these great kids like trophies."

The janitor laughed. "It's the American way. Give him credit."

"I'll give him all the credit he wants. I just want him to leave me alone."

The janitor looked at his watch. "I've got to get back home. Glad to help you, though. Thanks for the ten bucks." He stuck out his hand. " 'Luck, Alex."

"I'll send you a postcard, who knows where from. Maybe Canada. You've been a good buddy, Pete."

"Are you taking off right now?"

"Yep."

"Well, fasten your seat belt."

The boy watched the janitor cross the floor toward the stairs. The man turned and waved. "Turn the lights off when you go."

The boy stood quite still for a few minutes. The upstairs door slammed; a car started up and drove away. Alex noticed the basketball that Eddie and Stevie had forgotten to put away. He walked out onto the court with it and tossed it neatly through the basket.

In the darkness of the supply room Eddie and Stevie looked at each other. Stevie raised her eyebrows.

"Why not?" Eddie whispered.

Stevie took a deep breath and walked out into the gym. "Excuse me," she said, "would you like some passengers on your trip to Canada? As far as New Hampshire? We've got enough money for one tankful of gas."

As Alex stared at her in amazement, Eddie and Fawn came into the gym and stood next to Stevie.

"I'm being kidnapped by dwarfs," Alex said.

Chapter 10

"ARE YOU GUYS GHOSTS?" ALEX SAID.

"Yes," Eddie said. "So we wouldn't take up much room in your car. You do have a car, don't you?"

"Yes, I have a car. Seriously, are you running away from home? Because I've got problems enough without getting picked up for transporting runaway kids."

"It would take too long to tell you now," Stevie said. "We ought to get going before somebody comes in to see why the lights are on. We are not runaways. We missed a train connection. We really and truly need a ride to New Hampshire."

"Where in New Hampshire?"

"Well, that's part of the problem."

"I'll get our stuff." Eddie disappeared and came back with the plastic bag, Stevie's big paper bag, and her baseball bat. "We're ready."

With his hand on the electric light switches Alex paused and looked around the gym. "So long, childhood." He gave a hard kick to the basketball that lay on the floor.

60

As it bounced along the length of the court, he turned out the lights.

His car was a dark green Volvo wagon, four or five years old. The back was packed with camping gear: two sleeping bags, a folded tent, a parka, flashlights and Coleman lantern, fishing gear, a couple of blankets, a down-filled jacket, two suitcases, some books.

"You going to live in the wilderness or what?" Eddie said, taking it all in.

"I might," Alex said. "Me and Thoreau."

"Who's he?" Eddie said.

"A dude that liked to live in the woods by himself."

Stevie sat in front, and Eddie and Fawn sat behind them.

"You guys brother and sisters?" Alex started the car and they drove toward the main street.

"Eddie and Fawn are brother and sister," Stevie said. "I'm a friend." She felt shy with this boy, maybe because he was older, or maybe because he was so good-looking.

"When we get out on the highway, you can tell me the story. Right now I'm concentrating on leaving home. When I'm an old man, I'll try to remember what it was like when I finally cut loose, and if all I can remember is a bunch of kids I never saw before telling me their life story, how will I be able to write my autobiography?" He slowed down as they drove past a supermarket with a sign reading CARAS BEALE STREET MARKET—Open Twenty-Four Hours. "So long, slaves," he muttered.

A minute later he turned down a residential street and drove slowly past a big brick house with two pink plastic flamingos on the lawn. "So long, faithless woman. May

61

you marry John Barker and dwell in boredom and the country club all of your days." He speeded up, cut around the block, and back onto the street leading north out of town.

They drove in silence to the interstate, where Alex picked up speed. Stevie glanced at him out of the corner of her eye a few times. He looked grim, and he was sitting hunched forward over the steering wheel. She could tell he felt bad about leaving home. She wanted to tell him she knew the feeling, but he clearly didn't want to talk. His father must be a really mean man to throw him out just because he didn't want to go to college right away. She knew several people who had taken a year or two off between high school and college to find out what they really wanted to do.

She tried to think how she could tell him the story of Eddie and Fawn and herself without it turning into a long saga like *The Thousand and One Nights*. There was such a lot to explain. Not knowing where Uncle Tim lived made her sound like either an idiot or a liar, unless she could make him see how it had happened.

After a while Eddie said, "Excuse me, but is this actually your car?"

Startled out of whatever he'd been thinking about, Alex said, "What? Yeah, of course it is. Why?"

"Because there's a cop behind us, and you're a little over the speed limit. I thought if it was a hot car, you might be in trouble."

Alex laughed. "It's all mine, registered and paid for." He slowed down a little. "You're a practical kid." A minute later he said, "You'd better tell me where in New Hampshire you want to go. There's more than one route, you know."

Stevie sighed. "Well," she said. "It's a long story, but I don't know how to make it short and have it make any sense."

"We've got all night," he said. "All summer as far as I'm concerned. So shoot it to me."

Stevie began with the loss of the farm. When she got to the New York part, Eddie helped her out here and there. Alex made no comment and asked no questions.

When she had finished, Alex didn't speak for a few minutes. "It's complicated, all right," he said, "but I get it. Mine is a lot shorter. I have a considerably older sister and three brothers. The sister and two brothers are brilliant successes, and my old man values success more than anything. The third brother is in a group home for the retarded. My arrival on this planet was a mistake and a disaster. Two years later my mother divorced my father. I was supposed to be the most brilliant of all, to compensate the old man for Jerome and for my mother's splitting. Unfortunately I am not the kid he counted on. Ergo: I am getting myself out of his way. Maybe out of my own way. End of story."

"So here we are," Eddie said. "The Double Trouble Club."

"Or maybe the Survivors," Stevie said.

A very small voice from behind Stevie said, "I'm hungry."

"What am I thinking of!" Alex said. "You kids must

be starved. When did you eat last?" A minute later he took an off ramp into a cluster of gas stations and fast-food places. He turned into one where they could order from the car.

"We don't have much money," Stevie said, "and I want to buy a tank of gas."

"Don't worry about it. My sister was there when the old man and I had our fight. She stuck some money in my pocket. Order whatever you want."

They parked in the parking lot and ate in silence. When they had used the rest rooms and gone back to the car, Alex spread out one of the sleeping bags in a cleared space in back where Fawn could sleep.

"When we find a decent-looking campground or something, I'll pull off and we can all get some sleep," Alex said. "I didn't get much last night."

"Are you really going to Canada?" Stevie asked him.

"No. I didn't want the folks at home to know where to find me. I'll tell my sister, because she can keep a secret, but otherwise I want to be out of the mainstream." He paused. "So, you wonder where I'm going. I've been thinking about it. Let me think a little longer before I tell you. I've got kind of a crazy idea perking in my head."

About an hour later he turned into a small picnic area at the side of the road, drove into a space under a grove of trees, and stopped.

"Where are we, just out of curiosity?" Stevie asked.

"We just crossed over into New Hampshire."

She could hardly believe it. In the last few days, she had begun to think of New Hampshire as some mythical kingdom that mortals strove for but never reached. The smell of the pine trees and the soft night air seemed like heaven. And she wouldn't be awakened by the shattering clang of trash cans at five A.M.

Alex put down the second sleeping bag on the pine needles beside the car and went instantly to sleep. Eddie looked suspiciously at the woods beyond them and offered to sleep on the front seat so Stevie and Fawn could have the back.

"I'll take my bumps from the steering wheel and gearshift—not wild animals."

"Like chipmunks?" Stevie grinned at him.

"Like anything on four feet."

Stevie hadn't realized how tired she was. She fell asleep at once on the car seat, even though it was too short for her.

She came awake with a leap of terror as a bright light shone directly in her face. She held her hand up to her eyes, trying to see. Eddie was struggling to get his head out from under the steering wheel so he could sit up. Fawn was crying, and a stern voice was saying, "Up on your feet and put your hands on the car."

"Officer." Alex's voice sounded both sleepy and alarmed.

"You heard me. On your feet." The blinding light was on Alex now, as he struggled to his feet.

There were two highway patrolmen. One held the light on Alex while the second one frisked him. They pulled Eddie out and frisked him, too. Eddie looked scared. Stevie got out before they could order her to. Fawn climbed over the seat and stood close to Eddie.

One officer searched the car thoroughly while the other one took down the information on Alex's license and registration. He asked for ID from Stevie. She found her Iowa learner's permit. He frowned over it.

"You all related?" he said. "Iowa? Connecticut?"

"We three kids were on our way to New Hampshire to stay with our uncle because our dad is in Alaska on a job," Stevie said, "but we missed connections. Alex was driving to New Hampshire, so he gave us a ride."

The officer gave her a long, searching look. Then he crouched down beside Fawn. "Who's that boy?" he said, indicating Eddie.

"My brother Eddie," she said. She was nervous, but she gave him a smile.

"You like Eddie?"

"I love him."

"You like these other folks? They nice to you?"

"Oh yes," she said. "They're my friends."

The officer straightened up and patted Fawn's head. He looked at the other officer. "Clean?"

"Clean as a whistle. Where you heading for?" he said to Alex.

"North Lakeville."

"Okay. There's a rule against camping overnight in this picnic area."

"Oh. I didn't know that. We'll be on our way."

"Take it easy." The two men climbed into the patrol car, backed out onto the highway, and took off.

"Whew!" Alex mopped his forehead. "What a way to wake up."

66

"They were looking for dope," Eddie said. "And checking on you being a child-porno producer. Fawn saved the day."

"She sure did. Fawn, nobody could ever suspect you of lying. Not with that smile." Alex leaned down and patted the top of her head.

When they were getting into the car ready to leave, Stevie heard Fawn say, "What did I do, Eddie?"

"Remember how Gram used to tell you just to be your own sweet self?"

"I remember that."

"Well, that's what you were. And you got us out of a jam."

"Oh, good," she said.

Chapter 11

"EDDIE, STICK YOUR HEAD UP HERE SO WE CAN TALK."
Alex had the car back on the highway. "I have some
questions."

Eddie leaned his head on the front seat. "Fire away."

"If I get Stevie's story right, she's counting on her
uncle being willing to take in not only her but you and
Fawn."

"Not counting on," Stevie said. "Hoping. I don't even
know if he wants *me*. My father sprung it on him just
before we left."

"What kind of guy is he?"

"I never saw him. Neither has Dad since my uncle went
off to college. He and his wife have this dairy farm that
she inherited."

"What's she like, do you know?"

"I have no idea."

Alex thought for a minute. "Sounds like a long shot."

"Like about from here to Mars," Eddie said.

"And the main thing with you, Ed, is, you don't want to get separated from your sister."

"Don't want to, am not going to."

"Plus, Stevie, you don't know where this uncle is."

"It sounds like a mess, doesn't it?"

"Well, I've been thinking. Where I'm going is this place on a lake where I went every summer when I was a kid. It's my favorite place. But the camp went out of business, and now there's nothing there but the old recreation building. There's no road; you have to go in by boat, so it's not a hot item in the real-estate market. I called the bank to see if they'd let me stay there this summer for a small rental, plus I said I'd repair the rec building. They agreed, and that's where I'm headed."

Eddie and Stevie looked at each other.

"That sounds nice," Stevie said. "I hope you'll have a great summer."

He glanced at her. "You guys can stay there with me till you get straightened out, if you want to."

Stevie caught her breath. "You mean it?"

"You girls can bunk out in the rec building, and Eddie can share my tent."

"In the woods?" Eddie's voice sounded small.

"In the woods. You'll have to have your rhinoceros gun at the ready, but you won't mind that, will you? And a few tigers?"

"Don't laugh at him," Stevie said. "He's not used to the country."

"Eddie, there are deer in those woods, now and then a

moose, and if you go back far enough, a bear or two, but believe me, they're more scared of you than you are of them."

"Impossible," Eddie said.

"Don't leave food lying around. That's the only thing that might lure a bear. But in five summers there, I never saw a bear, and only one moose eating lilies at the end of the lake. The only time animals like that might be kind of ornery is in rutting season, and that's not in summer. Well, what do you say?"

Neither Eddie nor Stevie spoke for a moment, each trying to read the other's mind. Finally Fawn spoke up.

"I want to stay at Alex's," she said. "I like him."

"Then that's settled," Eddie said. "Fawn's the boss."

"As soon as I can get hold of my father," Stevie said, "he'll send me some money. But he may insist I go to Uncle Tim's right away." She paused. "And I don't want to."

"Worry about that later," Alex said. "I am hoping I can get a part-time job with the guy who owns the boat yard. What I really want to do is make wooden boats. This guy makes beautiful small boats, canoes, rowboats, small sailing boats. He does it the old way, all wood."

"What about money?" Eddie said. "Like, we don't have any."

"All we have to worry about is food. The lake is full of fish. There's a farm that sells vegetables cheap. Even if I don't get a job right off, I've got the money my sister gave me and a couple hundred of my own in a savings account. We'll survive."

"I don' .ike living on somebody else," Eddie said.

"Don't worry, you'll do your share. There's a lot of work to do on the place." He drove awhile in silence. "One more thing. Small-town people are apt to be nosy—not all of them, but some of them—especially about people 'from away,' as they say. And nowadays they think everybody's into drugs. Let's keep our story simple. You kids missed a connection with your relatives, Stevie's dad is in Alaska, I gave you a lift and a place to stay till you get connected. Okay?"

"And what are me and Fawn?" Eddie said. "Something that blew in off the street?"

"You're Stevie's friends. You were going with her to good old Uncle What's-His-Name and his forty-seven cows."

"Are we really?" Fawn had been listening intently.

"No, honey, you're going to spend at least some time with good old Uncle Alex and his forty-seven hang-ups," Alex said.

"Good," Fawn said. "I don't think I'd like cows."

The sky was beginning to turn gray in the east. Ahead of them in the distance the White Mountains loomed like a jagged wall of mist. There were other, lower mountains close by.

"The Ossipees," Alex said in answer to Stevie's question. "If it's still there, there's an all-night diner in Conway that has good coffee. I don't want to fall asleep driving."

"We all got problems," Eddie said.

Alex glanced back at him. "Do you resent me, Eddie?"

Eddie sank back in his seat. "I don't resent nobody."

He did though. He wasn't used to some dude he didn't even know making all the plans and giving the orders. Gram never bossed him around; they worked things out together. His eyes filled with tears, and he scrubbed at them with his fists. It would shame him more than he could stand if that big jock knew he had made Eddie cry. Anyway it wasn't him; it was not having Gram anymore. He didn't think he could bear it.

Fawn snuggled close to him. She always knew when he was feeling bad. She knew he cried sometimes over Gram. She had cried at first, but as far as he could tell, it didn't really sink in with Fawn that Gram was gone forever. She was too young to understand about death. Not that he dug it, either. How could she be there, making lentil soup for supper, joking about the dumb soap opera she'd just seen, and minutes later be lying on the floor with the light gone out of her like a blown-out candle?

"I'm sorry we're not making this drive in daylight," Alex was saying, "so you could see the Presidentials. New Hampshire has really neat mountains. They say the Rockies are pretty great, but I don't see how they could beat ours."

Ours, Eddie thought. They're his mountains, his car, his camp, his lake. We're being swallowed up by a Greek from outer space.

"My mother was born in Denver," Stevie said. "She loved the Rockies. We took a trip out there one summer when I was little. I couldn't get used to them. Where we live, you can see for miles, but mountains keep bumping into your eyes. Like the skyscrapers in New York."

Eddie wondered if Stevie missed her mother the way he missed Gram. She'd been dead three years, Stevie said; did it get better or worse? He couldn't tell from the way Stevie spoke. He liked Stevie. She was gentle. He smiled to himself. Except when she took it into her head to slam a baseball bat at a pusher.

Fawn had fallen asleep beside him by the time they came to Conway. "I'll stay here with Fawn," he said softly.

"We won't be long," Alex said. "I just need some coffee."

Eddie watched them go into the diner and sit at the counter. They were talking up a storm. He wondered if Stevie was getting a crush on the Greek. He was handsome, all right, must be six foot three, probably captain of the basketball team. He had that lopey knee-bending walk that jocks have. A car of his own, a chance to go to a good college. What a jerk, to throw it all away just because he got mad at his old man. Eddie and Fawn didn't even have an old man to get mad at. It was pretty weird when you thought about it, not knowing who your own father was. But maybe it was just as well. He didn't figure his mother would have been shacking up with a movie star or the Prince of Wales or any one of the Mets.

Fawn stirred, and he stroked her silky hair. "It's okay, baby. Everything's all right."

He touched the side of his head and went into his silent broadcast. It was easy to make up Gram's answers. EDDX3 to GRAM7, do you read me?

GRAM7 to EDDX3, reading you loud and clear.

Why's the world so screwed up anyway? I don't know what me and Fawn are going to do. Over.

It'll work out. It'll work out. . . .

GRAM7, you're fading. I can hardly hear you.

. . . work out . . .

Gram! Wait! But the voice had faded out.

Chapter 12

STEVIE FELT WIDE-AWAKE AFTER THE COFFEE. EDDIE and Fawn were asleep, and Alex had grown silent, driving more slowly now that they were in mountainous country. She wondered what he was thinking about. Maybe he regretted having taken on three kids. He had said in the diner that he was eighteen, and she knew that eighteen-year-olds looked on fourteen-year-olds as children. She wanted to tell him that in a few years, four years' difference would be just right.

Although the mountains so close made her uneasy, she liked the looks of the towns they were driving through. The sky was lightening, although the sun had still not cleared the tops of the mountains. The towns had narrow main streets and lots of shops and more motels and ski lodges and fast-food places than she would have expected.

In Jackson he pointed out the Falls and the hotel where his father had brought the family one summer. "He hates the country. I guess somebody told him it was what the proper American father would do." He shook his head. "He used to say to us, 'Don't be a box boy all your life.' That was how he started when he first came to this country. 'Get respect,' he'd say."

Eddie, awakened by the conversation, studied the waterfall. "Is that a government dam?"

"It's God's dam, kiddo. Or Mother Nature's or whoever."

Eddie frowned. He hated to be called kiddo. In a hostile tone he said, "When do we get to this so-called lake of yours?"

Alex didn't answer.

Stevie groaned inwardly. Let's don't make each other mad already; we've got enough grief without that. She knew Eddie felt patronized by Alex. None of this was going to be easy.

After a while Alex said, "We'd better stop in Gorham or Berlin and get some breakfast. The bank won't be open yet, but the guy I talked to said he'd leave the key with Tom Terry at the boat yard. I've already paid him the fifty bucks."

"Is there any furniture or anything?" Stevie asked, curious as to just what they were all getting into.

"He said there was some stuff the camp people left. Probably folding chairs, a long table, the kind of things that were there when I was. It won't be fancy."

"I hope there's beds." Eddie's voice sounded faraway.

Stevie glanced back. He had his head back against the seat, the neck of the Grinnell sweatshirt pulled up over half his face. Fawn's head was in his lap, and he had covered her with one of the blankets from the back of the car. Up here in the mountains the nights were cool.

"There are probably cots," Alex said. "If not, we'll have to get some at the army and navy store. I've got two sleeping bags."

"You mean we sleep on the ground?" Eddie said.

"You can leave, pal, any time the amenities don't come up to your standards," Alex said.

Stevie reached between the seats and touched Eddie's knee. "Cool it," she said. "Let's make a rule: You guys don't talk to each other till we've all had some breakfast and got to where we're going and had a chance to get some real sleep. Because if you two are going to make snide remarks to each other, I'm getting out of this car right now, and I'm not kidding."

No one spoke for a long time, not, in fact, until they were in Berlin and Alex had stopped in front of a café. "Let's eat," he said.

Except for ordering, nobody talked, partly from hunger and partly, to her surprise, because they were doing what she had told them to do. She wondered what she would have done if Alex had taken her up on getting out of the car back there on the empty road.

"I'm keeping track of how much of your money I spend," she told Alex, "so I can pay you back when my father sends me some money."

"Keep track for me, too," Eddie said. "I'll take it out in work, minimum hourly wage."

Alex looked down at him. "I'm sorry I snapped at you, Ed. Stevie's right, we're all too tired and tense."

"Sorry I was a brat," Eddie muttered.

Alex stuck out his hand. "Friends?"

"Sure, why not." Eddie shook the big hand. "How tall are you?"

"Six-two."

"I'm exactly five feet. That's my trouble. I'm a short man in a tall world."

Stevie laughed, but Alex answered him seriously. "I know how you feel. When I was your age, I had two brothers both six-three, and I was five-one, a hundred and thirty-eight pounds."

Eddie looked at him in astonishment. "For real?"

"For real. I bear the short man's scars to this day. But don't worry, all of a sudden you'll find yourself up there."

"I hope."

"I know. Look at your feet. You've got big feet. That's a sure sign."

On the rest of the drive to North Lakeville, Eddie admired the scenery, praised the pretty country road, pointed out sights to Fawn—"Look at that squirrel! Look at him zip up that tree!"

Stevie didn't point out that the squirrel was a chipmunk.

Chapter 13

IT WAS STILL FAIRLY EARLY WHEN THEY PASSED A SMALL painted sign on a hill that read North Lakeville.

"One paradise, coming up!" Alex sang out.

Fawn woke up and rubbed her eyes. "Where are we, Eddie?"

"Paradise, the man says. Otherwise known as North Lakeville. How you feel, Fawnsel?" He rubbed her head.

She yawned. "Sleepy."

They came over the top of a hill and down into the village.

"Thar she lays." Alex was excited. "Hasn't changed one iota in four years. Or forty."

Eddie looked at the narrow street in dismay. This was paradise? On the right a grassy slope led down to a lake with woods and distant mountains on the far side. On the left was the village proper: a tiny post office, a variety store, a store whose sign read Gavin's Supermarket Meats and Grocs. Next to Gavin's was Sandra's Spa, Sodas, Fishing Tackle, Papers, Misc. The last two buildings before the road curved east to follow the lakeshore were a small public library and a drugstore.

Just at the bend of the road, beyond the stores, there was a house and a boat yard, and past that the steeple of a small church.

Alex was smiling driving about ten miles an hour. "Well, what do you think?" he said.

"Where is the camp?" Stevie said.

"Across the lake, right where the shore makes a bend to the east. You can almost see the roof of the rec building through the trees. Prepare to turn yourself into a country bumpkin, Ed." Alex grinned as he looked at Eddie's dismayed face.

"There's no deli," Eddie said.

Alex laughed. "And no subway. No taxis."

"If there isn't any road around the lake," Stevie asked him, "how do we get over there?"

"We walk on water," Eddie said grimly. "This is paradise."

"Can you swim, Ed?" Then at Eddie's look of horror Alex said, "Only kidding. We go by boat. But can you swim?"

"Where would I swim? In the East River garbage?"

"All right, we'll have swimming lessons. You'd like to swim, wouldn't you, Fawn?"

"How do you do it?"

"Oh, you learn to use your arms and legs so you can go through the water like a fish. We'll get you guys swimsuits. You swim, don't you, Stevie?"

80

"I even have my suit," Stevie said. To Fawn she said, "Swimming is fun. You'll like it."

Alex drove into the yard of the house where the boat yard was and stopped the car. "It's early, but if I know the Terrys, they've been up an hour at least."

They heard the sound of a saw. The dock and the boat house were at the bottom of a sloping lawn. Two freshly painted rowboats were bottom up on the grass, and a big canoe was propped up on wooden horses, half-in and half-out of the boathouse.

A tall middle-aged man with thick gray hair came out of the boat house with a saw in his hand. He looked up at the car a moment and then climbed the slope. Alex got out.

"Help you?" the man said in a deep, pleasant voice.

Alex seemed suddenly shy. "I'm Alex Caras," he said. "Mr. Bement at the bank said—"

The man interrupted him. "Great day in the morning! You *are* Alex Caras. Man, you've grown three feet since I saw you last!" He pumped Alex's hand. "Great to see you, Alex. Sorry I didn't recognize you right off, but you're not the kid that used to hang over my shoulder and ask me why I was doing this, why I was doing that."

"I'll probably still hang over your shoulder." Alex introduced him to Stevie and to Eddie and Fawn.

Tom Terry's blue eyes searched each face as he shook hands with them all. "Mighty glad to meet you," he said. "It'll be good to have some folks staying over at the camp again." He turned and called toward the house. "Annette, come out and see who's here."

A small, dark, pretty woman came out, wiping her hands on a big apron. "Guess who this guy is," her husband said, putting his hand on Alex's shoulder.

She looked at him a moment and said in a strong French-Canadian accent, "The boy who love the boats. Alex, isn't it? But how beeg!" She measured about four feet with her hand. "I remember you like this, and a little plumper, eh?"

Alex laughed. "Quite a little plumper. Mrs. Terry, these are my friends." He introduced them.

"We are so glad you are here," Mrs. Terry said. "Now you will come in and have some real French pancakes, yes? With real New Hampshire maple syrup." She waved away Alex's comment that they had had breakfast.

Now come the questions, Eddie thought, trying to remember who he and Fawn were supposed to be and why they were here.

But in the big, good-smelling kitchen where everything shone with cleanliness, nobody asked questions. While Mrs. Terry fed them thin pancakes with melted butter and warmed syrup, Tom filled Alex in on the local news, who had died in the four years since Alex had been here, who had moved away.

"Old Man Gavin turned the store over to his son, but he still keeps an eye on it. We have a new librarian, a young woman from the university, bought herself the little cottage down by the cove. I told her she's going to get flooded out some spring, but she says she likes the view."

Eddie was glad to hear there was a library. Gram had always read aloud to them, and she had started teaching Fawn to read. He didn't want Fawn's education to slide backward up in this wild country. These Terrys seemed like okay people, the kind of folks Gram would have liked. Mrs. Terry paid a lot of attention to Fawn, and she sure made fantastic pancakes, almost as good as Gram's blintzes. He noticed how happy Alex looked. He was sorry he had snarled at him earlier. Alex was being very good to them, but Eddie believed in pysching people out before he trusted them too far. Stevie he had already made up his mind about. Stevie was all right.

Alex and Tom Terry went down to the boat yard to find an outboard that Alex could rent for the summer, an old one, Alex said, because he was a little low in funds.

Stevie was telling Mrs. Terry about her farm and about her father being in Alaska. She didn't tell about losing her train ticket or missing connections with her uncle. Stevie knew better than to spill everything to strangers, too. Eddie was feeling full of approval and full of pancakes. There was just one question he had to ask.

During a pause in the conversation he said as casually as he could, "They got bears over in those woods?"

Mrs. Terry didn't laugh. "There are a few, but they are not often where you see them. Unless people leave out garbage, they won't come around. I know how you feel, Eddie. I come here from Quebec when I marry Tom, and I never before seen even one bear except in the zoo. But if you walk in woods, make noise and the bear goes away.

He is afraid of people. And the deer are so beautiful, you will see."

Eddie nodded. It was good to talk to a city person for a change. Fawn had fallen asleep beside Mrs. Terry, who picked her up gently and held her in her lap. Fawn was sucking her thumb in her sleep. She'd done that a lot since Gram died.

"I am anxious to see a moose," Stevie was saying. "I've never seen one."

" 'I'd rather see than be one,' " Eddie said softly, and Mrs. Terry nodded and laughed. The lady had read the right books. "Fawn has never seen a cow, but she's sure they're scary."

"Purple or not, eh?" Mrs. Terry said.

Alex and Tom came back into the house to say that Alex had rented a boat. Tom Terry looked at Fawn asleep in his wife's arms and said, "Alex, why don't you and I take your gear across the lake and let the little girl sleep. She must be tired. You can pick them up on your second trip." To his wife he said, "Want me to lay her down on the bed?"

"No, let her be. It is nice to hold a child again."

"I would like to go to the post office," Stevie said, "while you're gone. I have to get a letter to my father. He'll be worried when he doesn't know where I am."

"I'll go with you," Eddie said. "Check out the town. If Fawn wakes up, will you tell her I'll be right back?"

Stevie and Eddie went out of the house just ahead of Alex and Tom Terry.

"Hey!" Eddie pointed to two boys on bikes. One of

84

them, about Eddie's age but taller and fat, was leaning in the open back window of the Volvo, poking around.

"Bubber!" Tom Terry yelled. "Get out of there!"

The boy ducked back so quickly, he bumped his head on the window frame. The other boy laughed and rode his bike down the street.

"What do you think you're doing?" Tom said.

"Uh, I thought it was an abandoned car," the boy said. "Out-of-state plates."

"Oh, get out of here." He kicked the back tire of the boy's bike.

"Hey!" The boy looked back angrily, glaring at Stevie and Eddie. He rode off down the street, muttering.

"That kid is a pain," Tom said. "Well, let's get at it." He opened the back of the Volvo and lifted out Alex's suitcases.

As Stevie and Eddie walked toward the stores and the post office, Alex ran after them and gave Stevie a five-dollar bill. "Get me a whole bunch of colored postcards, real gaudy ones, and a book of stamps, postcard rate, okay?"

Eddie grinned as Alex went back. "Going to swamp his girl with postcards? High-class stuff."

"Maybe they're for his retarded brother," Stevie said.

Eddie had forgotten about the brother. When they went into the drugstore, Stevie gave Eddie the money. "You find some. I have to get some stationery and a pen."

At the post office, the postmistress looked up from her sorting and smiled. "Hello. Lovely morning. I'm Myra Haines."

"I'm Stephanie Martin," Stevie said. "This is Edward Sanders."

"Welcome to town. You came with that nice Caras boy. I heard he'd rented the camp and I saw you go by."

"I have to write a letter," Stevie said. "Is it all right if I just write it here?" She pointed to the shelf that ran along under the window. There was a chain for a pen, but no pen attached to it.

"Have you got a pen?" Mrs. Haines said. "I try to keep one there, but they always disappear."

"Thank you, I have one." She opened the packet of stationery, carefully wrote the date and address, and then: "Chamber of Commerce, Valdez, Alaska. Dear Sirs: I have a problem. . . ."

While she was doing that, Eddie bought Alex's stamps.

"Are you a fisherman, Edward?" Mrs. Haines asked him.

Eddie was bewildered. "Fisherman? I'm only twelve years old."

Mrs. Haines didn't laugh. She said, "That was a dumb way for me to put it. I meant do you like to fish? The reason I asked—since my husband died, I have trouble finding somebody to go fishing with me, and I hate to go alone. So I'm always looking for somebody who likes just sitting out there in a boat and tossing a line in and relaxing."

"I get it." For a minute there he'd thought the woman was batty. "The only fish I ever saw all in one piece were in the fish market, and they were dead as a doornail."

"You're from the city."

"Brooklyn."

"Oh yes. My husband and I once went to the Brooklyn Academy of Music. Years ago."

Eddie was excited. He'd almost begun to think of Brooklyn as something he'd invented in his dreams. "Gram took me there once to hear some guy read his poetry. He was from Kiev, and she was, too."

"Was it good poetry?"

"I didn't understand it too well, but Gram cried. We shook the guy's hand afterward."

Mrs. Haines glanced up as someone came in, but Eddie was so intent on having found a kindred soul who had been to Brooklyn, he didn't notice. "The guy was a Jewish refugee. Gram was Jewish."

"What do you want, Bubber?" Mrs. Haines said sharply.

"Just cruisin' around," Bubber said.

"Well, cruise somewhere else. This is government property."

Eddie turned his head and saw the same two boys. They didn't look friendly, but he couldn't be bothered with them.

"If it's gov'ment property, what's *he* hangin' around here for?" Bubber said.

"He happens to be buying stamps, not that it's any business of yours. Run along now, before I get cross."

Taking their time, the boys sauntered out and then rode their bikes up and down the sidewalk in front of the post office.

Mrs. Haines sighed. "Some people in this town are the salt of the earth. Some, on the other hand, are not."

"Excuse me," Stevie said, "what is the zip code here?"

Mrs. Haines gave it to her.

"And would you happen to know the one for Valdez, Alaska? I hate to bother you."

"That's what I'm here for." Mrs. Haines flipped through the zip code book and read it off.

"I can't afford Express Mail, but what would be the next quickest way to get a letter to Alaska?"

Mrs. Haines suggested registered mail, return receipt. "Not necessarily all that much faster but it gets attention all along the way."

Eddie could see how relieved Stevie was when she finally got a letter off to Alaska. He didn't think it was such a sure thing that it would ever reach her father, but he understood that having done *something* made her feel better.

The two boys on the bikes were hanging around in front of the drugstore, and the boy called Bubber said something that made the other boy laugh, but Eddie didn't hear him and didn't want to. They were just a pair of smart-ass kids, the kind you find everywhere. He was thinking about Mrs. Haines. That was a nice woman.

"Do you know how to fish?" he said to Stevie.

"Sure."

"Will you teach me?"

"Sure. Why?"

"Oh," he said in his most throwaway manner, "me and the post-office woman are going fishing."

Chapter 14

STEVIE WATCHED EDDIE'S FACE AS THEY PREPARED TO get into the boat. He was trying hard not to look scared, but when Tom Terry lifted Fawn in beside Stevie in the stern and the boat rocked, she saw Eddie clap his hand to his mouth to keep from yelling in alarm.

It would have been funny if he hadn't been so frightened: this street-smart kid who roamed around Manhattan, dodged druggies and muggers, rode the subway, and managed to survive as if it were all a normal experience—which of course it was for him—was now scared to death to get into a perfectly safe broad-bottomed outboard to cross a calm lake.

Alex had given him a life preserver, which had alarmed him even more.

"It's the same as wearing a seat belt in a car," Stevie told him, as she showed him how to put it on. "I think it's the law now."

Annette Terry was packing cleaning things into the bow: a broom, a mop, a bucket, dust cloths, liquid soap. She had offered to come help them clean, but Alex had talked her out of it.

"I'm a good housekeeper," he told her. "We never could keep a housekeeper long after my mother left, my dad was such a crab to work for. So from the age of about ten I became a very good housemaid, cook, nurse, and all-around cleanup kid."

Stevie wondered how long his retarded brother had lived at home. That must have been hard. She wondered if Alex saw his mother often. There were a lot of things she'd like to know about him.

Tom Terry held the boat steady as Eddie got in. His weight tipped the boat to one side, and Fawn gave a little yip of alarm.

"Balance your weight," Tom said. "Hold on to the gunwales."

"Grab the sides and step in the middle," Stevie said. How did Tom expect Eddie to know what a gunwale was when he'd never been in a boat in his life?

Tom gave her a quick grin and said, "Touché."

Annette was laughing. "Tom think everybody grow up in a boat, eh? He was the same with me. You and me, Eddie, we are city kids, right?"

"Right." Eddie half sat, half fell onto the seat and gave Annette a weak smile.

These are nice people, Stevie thought. If everybody in town is as nice as the Terrys and the woman at the post office, things will be fine. She thought of Bubber, but he was just a kid, and as her mother used to say, there's one rotten apple in every barrel.

They said good-bye to the Terrys, Tom pushed the boat away from the dock, and Alex started the motor. It made a pleasant chugging sound as the boat moved slowly out into the lake. She thought Eddie looked relieved, although he still held on to the edge of his seat. Perhaps he had pictured one of those racing inboards, a Gar Wood or something, tearing through the water throwing up a tower of waves.

She looked back and waved to the Terrys on the dock. They looked smaller as the boat moved away from the shore. From here she could see the bend of the lake as it swung around to the east. The camp must be about there, on that point, where the woods came down almost to the water. Behind the forest a series of low mountains joined together, the trees thinning out toward the tops. There was no wind, and the bright blue sky was reflected in the quiet water. No wonder Alex liked it so much; it was beautiful.

She turned Fawn's head and pointed to a loon, some way down the lake. As they watched, the bird dived, then came up several minutes later, a distance from where she had gone down.

"It's a loon," she told Fawn. "She's diving for fish. They can stay underwater a long time."

"Do you have them in Iowa?" Alex asked above the noise of the motor.

She shook her head. "I saw one once on one of the Great Lakes; I think it was the time we went to Duluth."

"They were in that movie," Eddie said, "*On Golden Pond.* Remember, Fawn, that was Gram's favorite movie that year."

Fawn shook her head.

"That's right, you were too little." Eddie sounded sad, as if sharing the memory with Fawn would have made it better.

"That picture was shot in New Hampshire," Alex said. He turned the boat, heading for the point of land where the camp was.

No one spoke on the rest of the ride. An old dock, partly crushed by winter ice, came into view. Alex pointed toward it and slowed the boat. It was hard to see much because of the trees, but now Stevie could see the low roof of what must be the recreation building. If you weren't looking for it, you probably wouldn't see it at all.

Now she could see a path that ran along beside the lake, and another one that wound through a thick clump of pines toward the recreation building. Right on shore, near the dock was the pile of stuff Alex and Tom Terry had brought out on the first trip over. She noticed that Eddie was looking suspiciously at the dense woods that lay behind the camp. She knew he was thinking *bears*.

Alex eased the boat into the cove, cut the motor, and grabbed the edge of the dock.

"Are we there?" Fawn said.

"We're there!" Alex sounded excited. He climbed out and held the bow steady while the others got out. Then he hitched the rope to the dock piling and said, "Let me show you what's here before we unload the stuff we brought and carry everything up." He took off up the path toward the recreation building, almost running.

Eddie looked around him. "Is this place safe?" he said.

"It's a lot safer than Times Square, Eddie," Stevie said.

"Yeah, but I like to *know* what to look out for." Holding Fawn's hand tightly, he picked his way along the path behind Stevie.

"Oh, look," she said, pointing to a clump of tall bushes laden with berries. "Blueberries." She picked one.

"Watch it!" Eddie said. "They could be poisonous."

"Eddie, they're wonderful fresh-from-the-vine blueberries, two-fifty a box in New York, I'll bet."

"Can I have some?" Fawn said.

"Wait and see if Stevie drops dead." Eddie grinned. "You think I'm kidding?"

"No, I don't," Stevie said, "but I'm glad to be of service. Like the king's taster." She picked a handful and gave the berries to Fawn.

"Wash them first," Eddie said. "They're probably loaded with pesticides."

"Eddie!" Stevie wailed. "Who sprayed them? God?"

"Acid rain," Eddie said.

They came up the broken step of the recreation building and joined Alex, who was standing in the open doorway. At first it was hard to see anything. The lake side of the building had big windows without glass but covered with hinged wooden shutters that kept out the light. On the forest side several small, high windows let in what little light there was.

"Well," Alex said, "this is the rec building."

Eddie picked up two shingles that lay on the ground. "Do you spell that *w-r-e-c-k?*"

"You don't get the Ritz for the summer for fifty bucks."

Eddie peered past him. "You could have gotten this for twenty."

Alex stepped inside. "All it needs is a good cleaning. Look at that fireplace, you guys. Is that a fireplace or is that a fireplace?"

Eddie looked at the enormous fieldstone fireplace that angled across the lakeside corner. "That's a fireplace," he said. "Who chops the wood?"

"You." Alex clapped Eddie on the back. "Look on the bright side, man! We've got a place to hang out all summer, a beautiful lakeside camp with nobody to hassle us."

"I guess you're right," Eddie said. "It beats the Cocaine Plaza, right, Stevie?"

"I think it's great," Stevie said. "Let's get it cleaned out, and then we can move our stuff in. Look, what's all that stuff on the stage?"

At the far end of the long building a small stage was nearly covered with stacked-up furniture. They went down to look. There were about twenty folding chairs piled one on top of another; a long trestle table lying upside down; and piles of things covered with a tarp.

"Ed, help me open the shutters," Alex said. The two went outside, and a few minutes later light poured into the building.

"Oh, my!" Stevie said. She hadn't realized how dirty the place was. The floor was littered with dead pine needles, dried mud, and the droppings of small animals.

"Squirrels," Alex said, coming in. "They come down the chimney." He peered up inside the fireplace chimney. "Somebody boarded up the top of the chimney, but the

94

boards have been shoved aside. It's hard to keep out red squirrels. Well, we'll have to clean that out." He stepped back, his hands and one side of his face streaked with soot.

"What about water?" Eddie said.

"Eddie, that's a lake out there. Water, remember?"

"But even a dude like me knows you don't drink lake water," Eddie said.

"You're right." Alex pushed his hair back, leaving another smudge on his forehead. He looked tired. "There's a spring down around the bend, just beyond the cove where we swim. We carry the spring water to drink, use lake water to wash."

"I have to go to the bathroom," Fawn said softly.

"Well, we actually have one. A chemical flush toilet, and Tom gave me some chemical."

For the rest of the day they worked, stopping only long enough to eat the sandwiches Annette had made for them. Eddie and Alex had a long struggle putting up two of the four-man tents left by the camp owners. They were heavy, and getting up the ridgepoles took a lot of time with frustrating failures.

While the boys were working on the tents, Stevie swept and mopped, and Fawn helped by dusting everything she could find. It was Fawn who discovered the folded canvas cots piled in a dark corner. Stevie was relieved. Alex had the two sleeping bags and several old blankets, but she had not been looking forward to sleeping on the floor.

"Let's take a break and tell the boys what you found," she said to Fawn.

They walked along the path, past the dock, past the

sandy cove where a big barbecue grill had been cemented into the ground, around the curve of the path to the row of tent platforms. One tent was up, but Alex stood in front of the second one, his hands on his hips. The tent was a heap of canvas on the platform floor, and Eddie was nowhere to be seen.

"Where's Eddie?" Fawn said. "Eddie!"

Alex pointed silently. Eddie's head appeared from beneath the canvas.

"Eddie," Fawn said, "what are you doing under there?"

"The tent collapsed," Alex said, "just as we had it almost up. For the fifth time."

Eddie crawled out, looking disgusted and disheveled. "Camp life," he said. "Nature. Paradise." His hair hung over his eyes.

"Why didn't you holler?" Stevie said to Alex. "Three of us can do it easier than two." She started lifting one end of the tent.

Even with three of them, it took awhile.

"Why do we need two tents anyway?" Eddie said, when they finally got it in place. "One is big enough to hold an army."

Alex didn't answer, but Stevie knew, or thought she did, why they had to have two. Alex wanted some privacy.

At the end of the afternoon the rec building was relatively clean, Alex's huge thermos jug was full of spring water, Annette's bucket had been refilled with washing water, the beds were in place—Fawn's and Stevie's close together down at the stage end of the hall—and the big trestle table had been set up with four folding chairs.

Alex had brought two Coleman lanterns and several big flashlights and a two-burner Coleman stove.

"You really must have planned this trip," Stevie said. "You thought of everything."

"I was going to come anyway. The fight with my old man just speeded things up." He looked at his watch. "I forgot to get food. I'll make one more run to the village before it gets dark."

"You want one of us to go with you?" Stevie said.

Alex shook his head. "Why don't you guys go down to the cove and take a dip? The water's cold but it'll make you feel good. The bottom's sandy there, and the slope-off is gradual. But before I forget it, let me lay down a law: Don't anybody go in swimming alone, ever, and if you go in anyplace but the cove, bear in mind the land shelves off real steep everywhere else. It's way over your head, but not deep enough to dive. Okay?"

When he had gone, Stevie changed into her swimsuit and stripped Fawn down to her underpants and T-shirt. Eddie joined them at the beach, but he couldn't be persuaded to wade in any further than knee deep.

He wrapped his arms around himself and shivered. "It's icy!"

Fawn happily splashed and jumped up and down, shrieked, and threw water at her brother.

Although the water was cold, it felt good to Stevie after the heat and dust of cleaning. She swam out into the lake, enjoying the chance to use muscles that hadn't had any exercise since she left Iowa. She thought of her friends at home, the ones she usually swam with. The lake they went to was about a tenth the size of this one, and the water was never very cold at this time of year.

She came back to the beach gasping and glowing. Eddie had retreated to the warm sand, where he sat watching.

"How can you stand the cold?" he said to Stevie.

"As soon as you start swimming, you warm up. I'll treat you to a pair of swim trunks next time we go to the village," she said, "and Alex or I will teach you. It really makes you feel wonderful."

"Teach me too?" Fawn said.

"Of course. You're almost swimming already. Look, put your face underwater for a second so you won't be scared of it. Hold your breath, count to five, and then come up, okay? I'll hold on to you."

Eddie watched them for some time, shivering, his arms wrapped around his knees. Fawn was not afraid of the water, and in a short time she was learning how to kick with her face in the water and her arms straight out in front of her.

"That's enough for today," Stevie said finally. "We'll have a lesson every day, okay?"

"Yes!" Fawn was excited. "Eddie, I can swim!"

"You're doing great." Eddie's teeth chattered. "I guess I'll have to learn just so I can keep up with you."

"Eddie, you're freezing. Go put on some dry clothes," Stevie said.

He made a face. "Yes, Mother."

Later when they had picked and eaten some blueberries, Eddie eating with an air of one expecting instant death, he said, "You want to see my tent?"

98

They walked along the path to the tents. In Alex's tent the clothes and gear were strewn untidily, but Eddie's was very neat. The one cot looked lost in the tent meant for four people, but he had unpacked his few clothes and arranged them neatly folded on an uneven board set upon two rocks. His grandmother's mezuzah hung from the front tent pole, swaying slightly in the breeze.

Stevie praised his tidiness.

"Gram made us pick up after ourselves," he said. "She liked things neat." He paused. "The only thing is, how do I know in the middle of the night a bear won't walk in?"

Stevie looked at him and realized how young he was. Twelve was an in-between age, part child, part beginning to be grown up. Eddie sounded so competent and self-assured most of the time, she hadn't thought about how scary life could seem to him, especially when he had just lost his beloved grandmother and had no idea what was to become of Fawn and himself. She wished she could hug him and console him the way she could Fawn. Spending the night in this big, exposed tent on the edge of a forest that alarmed him even in daylight was going to be very frightening for him.

"I wish I could sleep in Alex's tent, I mean just sleep in there and have this one to keep my things in, but he wants to be alone."

"I think he needs to be alone as much as you need not to be."

"Well, I guess I'll survive," he said.

Stevie walked around the tent. "Roll down the back and

99

the sides, and you can close the front, too, at night. That's what you do when it rains." She looked at him. "I'm sure no bear is going to walk into a tent with someone in it, but I know how you feel, all exposed like that."

"Do you?" He looked anxious for her understanding. "Alex thinks I'm a wimp."

"I'm sure he doesn't, but he may not understand because this is a place he knows so well. If he had to spend the night on a Manhattan subway grate, *he* would be scared."

"So would I."

"Listen, how about this: Fawn and I are setting up our bedroom at one side of the stage. It's close to the bathroom, for one thing, and we can make kind of a cozy little room there. What if we put one of the extra cots in front of the fireplace, near the door, and you could sleep there if you get to feeling nervous here. That hall is so long, we wouldn't even hear you come in."

Eddie thought about it. "Alex will think I'm nuts."

"Oh, nuts to Alex," Stevie said impatiently. "No, I don't mean that, but we don't have to get his approval for everything we do. I'll speak to him. He'll see that going from a city like New York to an empty tent on the edge of a forest is a culture shock."

Eddie looked relieved. "Thanks, Stevie. After I've been here a little while, I won't feel so spooked, all right?"

"Anyway, Fawn will feel better at first to have you nearby. I'll tell Alex that."

So they got out one more cot, dusted it off, and set it in front of the fireplace. Stevie found a three-foot-high birch stump behind the building that she and Eddie dragged in and set in front of the cot like a footstool. She got some pine branches and arranged them like a center-piece in the middle of the table. "I hope Alex thinks to get some dishes and forks and spoons and cooking pots."

"He's got a stack of cooking pots that fit into each other," Eddie said. "I unpacked them. He must have been a Boy Scout or something." He shook his head. "Surviving in the country and surviving in the city are about as much alike as cheesecake and granola."

"And surviving on a farm is different from either one." Stevie cocked her head. "I think I hear the boat."

They ran down to the dock and watched Alex come in. He waved. He looked just right out there alone in that boat, Stevie thought; as if that was where he was meant to be. She couldn't picture him being a doctor or a lawyer or working for I.B.M.

He had brought a five-gallon can of kerosene, two big jugs of drinking water, a set of plastic dishes and cutlery, a lot of food, and a bag of charcoal briquettes for the barbecue.

"And," he said, when they had finished unloading, "presents for everybody." He tossed a small flat package at Eddie and one to Fawn, a thicker one toward Stevie. Eddie's was a pair of tan swimming trunks, Fawn's was a blue tank suit, and Stevie's was two paperback books, an English mystery and a novel about a girl growing up on a farm in South Dakota.

"Sorry," he said, "but they were fresh out of Iowa."

He admired the way they had fixed up the rec building, and when Stevie said casually that Eddie might sleep on the extra cot until Fawn got used to the camp, he just nodded.

While Eddie helped Alex build up a fire in the barbecue pit, Stevie made a salad from the vegetables Alex had brought back. They ate sitting on the sand, watching the sun disappear behind the mountains, the lake reflecting the soft pinks and lavenders of the sky.

Alex had unearthed his radio-cassette player from the back of the car, and they listened to his new *Showboat* tapes.

Fawn pointed to a loon out on the lake. They played a game of guessing where the big ungainly bird would surface and how long she would stay underwater. Alex told them how loons sometimes scream in the night like a woman in pain.

Behind them the woods grew blacker. Eddie glanced back nervously once or twice.

Some time after Fawn and Stevie had gone to bed, Stevie saw Eddie appear in the doorway carrying a flashlight and a blanket. He was wearing shorts and the Grinnell sweatshirt. She heard the faint scrape of the cot in front of the fireplace. The flashlight went out, and a stillness settled over the camp.

She was half-asleep when she heard an owl and a few minutes later the soft, quick patter of a squirrel or chipmunk running across the roof.

She fell asleep and woke later to a sound she couldn't identify at first. She listened. It was Eddie, and he was crying, so quietly she could barely hear him. She wanted to talk to him, to tell him everything would turn out all right. But she couldn't do that. When she was Eddie's age, her mother had already been dead a year, but if people had tried to tell her that everything was going to be all right, she would have felt like hitting them. You didn't get over things; you learned to live with them. And it was much too soon for Eddie to find any comfort in that.

She lay still, listening until the crying stopped.

Chapter 15

BY THE END OF THE FIRST WEEK THEY HAD FALLEN INTO a more or less regular routine. After breakfast they worked on the things that needed fixing: Alex was discovering that Eddie had a knack with hammer and nails, so the two of them worked on repairing the dock until it had reached the point where Eddie could finish it alone. Stevie climbed a tree and swung onto the roof to replace shingles that had blown off in the past two years. She had done that more than once on the barn at home. Alex repaired the front step to the rec building, and then built a couple of crude armchairs out of fallen boughs and chunks of wood.

Fawn helped wherever she could. One of her regular chores was to dust the rec-building furniture and sweep the pine needles that seemed to drift in overnight.

At noon they went for a swim. Alex was teaching Eddie, and Stevie was teaching Fawn, although Fawn caught on so fast, there was not much Stevie had to tell her. Eddie was slower. At first he hated putting his face in the water, but once he got used to that, he learned quickly.

"You're built for it," Alex told him. "You've got a good, neat body, all muscle, no fat."

Eddie beamed with pleasure.

They had a pickup lunch, everyone for himself, and in the afternoon they usually went to the village, Stevie looking for some word from her father. Alex had shown her and Eddie how to run the outboard. He always dropped in at the Terrys', even if only for a few minutes. Sometimes he ran errands for them in his car: vegetables to be bought from the farmer's roadside stand just north of town, or a trip to Gorham or Berlin to get materials that Tom needed. Tom quite often let Alex help him with the forty-year-old Old Towne canoe he was restoring.

On the days when the library was open, Stevie and Fawn and sometimes Eddie went there. They had taken out cards. The young librarian, fresh out of library school, seemed to enjoy talking to them.

"This isn't much of a reading town," she said, "except for Mrs. Haines and the Terrys and the Reverend Fuller."

The nameplate on her desk said Diana Blaine, and she said she was from Portland, Maine. When they were out of her hearing, Eddie referred to her as the Maine Blaine, but they liked her. She seemed lonesome.

The people they met on the street sometimes nodded, sometimes looked away, but almost never spoke. Stevie could tell, though, that they were curious about the four of them. Quite often one or two men in a boat stopped to fish within sight of the camp.

"They're checking up on us," Eddie said. "They think we're running a drug operation here. Stevie and Fawn grow the coke plants, Alex turns it into crack, and I push it."

She knew he was joking, but Stevie, too, had the feeling that they were being watched.

"I worry about Diana Blaine," Mrs. Haines said to Stevie one morning. Stevie liked to talk to Mrs. Haines; she was the only one except the Terrys with whom she felt comfortable. "She's a stranger here, and people in this part of the world aren't all that forthcoming to strangers. I've had her to dinner, and she and the Terrys and I have had some bridge games, but she ought to meet people her own age. I wish Yankees weren't so darned standoffish."

"They're curious about us," Stevie said.

"You bet they are. They can't figure out who belongs to who."

There was no one else in the post office, and no one coming down the street. Stevie decided it would be a good time to explain to Mrs. Haines just what the relationships were. "I'd like to tell you how we happen to be here," she said.

"Well, I'd love to hear anything you want to tell me, but don't feel obliged to tell me anything. I'm just as curious as anybody else, but I also respect people's privacy."

"I'd like to tell you." Making it as brief as she could, she told her how the threads of their lives had come together.

Mrs. Haines's expressive face was full of sympathy. "What a godsend that you happened to bump into Alex."

"Yes. I don't know what we would have done." Stevie paused. "Or what we'll do. Alex can't be expected to carry us forever. If I could just talk to my father, I'm sure I could make him understand that I'm not going to leave Eddie and Fawn, no matter what. They're too young. I don't understand why I haven't heard from him."

Mrs. Haines leaned her elbows on the counter and looked thoughtful. "It's likely that by now he knows you didn't connect with your uncle. Now, if that were me, if you were my child, what would I do?"

"Maybe he thinks I just ran away. Only I don't think he would."

"You're not the type. He would surely know that." She reached under the counter and brought up a phone book. "If he reported you missing, there'd be a report out. 'Course there are so many missing kids these days . . ." She was leafing through the phone book. "I'm going to call Joe McCord. He's a friend of mine over to the highway patrol office. He might have heard something." She dialed the number and asked for Officer McCord. "Well, ask him to call Myra Haines at the post office in North Lakeville when he comes in, will you?" She hung up. "It's a start."

"I hadn't thought about Missing Persons. Thank you very much." Stevie felt a load roll off her shoulders. Mrs. Haines seemed so competent.

As Eddie and Fawn came into the post office, Eddie looked upset. He had his knife in his hand, unopened. Once inside, he put it in his pocket.

"That mean boy called Eddie bad names," Fawn said.

"Never mind, Fawn." Eddie tried to smile. "Sticks and stones will break our bones, but who cares from names?"

"What mean boy?" Mrs. Haines looked out the window and saw Bubber and two of his friends saunter by. "Bubber. It figures. Unfortunately his mother's just as mean as he is, though I shouldn't say so. Just ignore him, Eddie. He's trash. And when are we going fishing?" When Eddie smiled but didn't answer, she said, "How about tomorrow afternoon around four? I get a half holiday tomorrow."

"Cool," Eddie said. "Only I don't know how."

"You will when I get through with you. I'll pick you up about four." She turned away as a woman came in to get her mail.

After the woman had gone, Eddie ran back to say, "I don't have a fishing pole."

"I'll bring you one. My back hall is full of them."

Later when they were at the Terrys' and Eddie was talking about fishing, Alex said, "You don't call it a fishing pole. It's a rod."

Alex had bought an old homemade canoe from Tom for five dollars and he was fixing it up so they could use it.

"Pole, rod, what's the difference?"

"Huck Finn fished with a pole. A pole is a whittled-down tree limb with a hook on the end. A rod is a work of art, made by craftsmen, aluminum and stainless steel and fiberglass. Mine is a telescoping spin rod with zoom-cast spinning reel. It telescopes to seventeen inches and weighs just over three ounces. You can spring it open in a second."

"Are you their salesman or what?" Eddie watched Alex carefully smooth the hull of the canoe with fine sandpaper.

"Nope, but I love my fishing rod."

108

"You can catch just as big a fish with Huck Finn's pole," Tom said, teasing Alex. "Don't let this dude snow you, Eddie." He and Alex had fallen into the easy relationship of two people working side by side.

Later they went up to the house for one of Annette's excellent suppers: codfish hash with potatoes and beets in a cream sauce with small bits of salt fat pork fried crisp, and hot johnnycake. Tom said, "Alex, I've been meaning to ask, now the summer trade's picking up, you want to work for me three days a week?"

Alex dropped the chunk of butter he'd been about to spread on his johnnycake. "You mean it?"

"I mean it. Long hours, lousy pay, hard work. I don't know many as would want it. I figured it would take a boat freak like you."

"I want it," Alex said. His dark eyes shone. "I want it, I want it."

Tom laughed. "You got it."

Eddie watched Alex's face with envy. He wished he was old enough for a job, and he wished he knew something he loved to do as much as Alex loved working on boats.

Tom was telling them about a school in wooden boat building over on the Maine coast, in Brooklin. "Guys come from all over the world, even from Africa where they always made their dugout canoes from tree trunks. They were worrying about using up all the suitable trees, so they came clear to Maine to find out if there was a better way. Maybe you could go over there in the fall, when things slow down here, and take that course. You'd come out a real master craftsman, better than I could teach you."

"Sounds good," Alex said, "but right now I'm too excited about working for you to think ahead."

"Don't think ahead." Eddie had said it aloud without meaning to. It was just what he was thinking. They all looked at him, and for a moment no one spoke. He tried to laugh it off. "My gram used to say, 'Wear life like a new sweater. Don't worry about the day it's going to unravel, 'cause if it's a good job of knitting, it could last you forever.' "

"I remember her saying that," Fawn said. She looked surprised, as if her grandmother had suddenly come alive for a moment.

"I'd like to have known your grandmother," Stevie said.

"If she was here right now," Fawn said, "she'd make you laugh."

Annette got up suddenly with tears in her eyes and retreated to the kitchen to get another plate of hot johnnycake. "Who wants more milk?" She came back with the pitcher. "I bet you don't drink enough milk over there. How do you keep things cold?"

"Alex got one of those zinc-lined wooden milk boxes from Mr. Gavin," Eddie said, relieved that Annette had changed the subject. He couldn't think what had made him burst out with that about Gram. "He buries it in the sand just below the water level in the cove. And I'm here to tell you, that water's cold!"

"Eddie turns blue when he swims," Fawn said. "His teeth chatter. I don't turn blue."

110

"That's 'cause you're smarter than I am, smartie." Eddie made a face at her.

"Girls are always smarter," Fawn said, and giggled.

They had Indian pudding with ice cream on top for dessert.

"For a goy, you are the best cook I ever ran across," Eddie said to Annette. He and Stevie helped her clear the table and do the dishes. "When my grandfather was alive, Gram let him do the cooking on Sundays. He almost always did corned beef and cabbage. He was Irish," he explained as Annette looked puzzled.

"Irish and Jewish," she said. "That is a wonderful mixture."

"That Bubber kid called me a Canuck today. What's a Canuck?"

Annette frowned. "It is a not-nice name for French Canadian."

"Well, I figured if Bubber said it, it wasn't nice. I told him I was an Irish Jew or a Jewish Irishman, he could have his pick. That really confused him." He laughed. "I called him Blubber, and that made him mad."

"He is trouble, that boy. His mother is worse." Annette scrubbed the frying pan extra hard. "She has a group, what do you call it, a clique?"

Stevie smiled. "In Iowa we say *click*. I wish I knew real French."

"I will teach you if you like," Annette said. "Only in France they laugh at the Canadian accent."

"I'd love to have you teach me."

"Maybe Fawn could come, too?" Eddie said. "I want her to be real educated."

"Of course. You too, Eddie, if you want. I love to teach. Here they look down on French, you know."

"Here they seem to look down on most everybody," Stevie said. "Nobody downtown has much to say to us. Just you and Mrs. Haines and the librarian."

"I know. Stay twenty or thirty years and they will start to say 'allo. Just now they begin to talk to me a little."

Eddie sprawled in the bow of the boat as it followed the path of moonlight back to camp. He was glad Alex had gotten that job.

He touched the little place on his temple, the key to his silent closed-circuit broadcast to Gram.

EDDX3 calling GRAM7, do you read me?

GRAM7 to EDDX3, reading you loud and clear. Whadda ya know for sure? GRAM7 over.

EDDX3 here. Don't know a thing for sure, but you always said nobody did. Fawn's going to learn French, me too, I guess. You said a person could never know too much. Right? Over to you.

GRAM7 back at you. Especially Jewish people because knowledge makes you strong, and us Jews need to be strong more than most people, on account of people like Hitler. Over to you, EDDX3.

That obnoxious Bubber kid called me a kike and a Jewboy today, and I thought about pulling out my switchblade and scaring the stupid jerk. But you know what popped into my head? Like how some Jewish kids call their grandmothers Bubba, and that sounds like the way these New Englanders say Bubber, and I nearly fell over laughing. "Go home, Grandmother," I said. "Go home, you dumb fake grandmother." He thought I'd gone nuts. But he went away.

GRAM7 to Edward, you listen to me, Edward Sanders. You get rid of that switchblade, and I mean now. Talk about dumb ignorant stupid! You hear me? Over.

EDDX3 to GRAM7. I hear you talkin'. Over and out.

Eddie slipped the knife out of his pocket and let it trail in the water in his hand for a moment, and then let it go. Too bad; he'd given five bucks and six baseball cards for that knife. But you didn't argue with Gram.

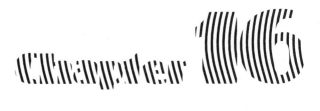

Chapter 16

STEVIE AND FAWN WERE BROWSING AROUND THE STACKS in the library. Eddie left them and wandered up the road that led out of town. He scuffed the dust with the toes of his sneakers. It hadn't rained for a while, but today you could smell rain in the air. Eddie couldn't remember smelling rain in New York, maybe because there were so many other smells.

He passed the roadside vegetable stand where Alex bought fresh vegetables. The field and gardens stretched out behind the neat white house. Stevie said her farm in Iowa was about twenty times as big as this.

The man at the stand was arranging rows of cabbages. A white cat sat at the end of the long table watching him. The man looked at Eddie and said, "Afternoon."

Wow! Eddie thought, a talkative Yankee!

He said, "Afternoon," politely and went over to the stand. "That's a nice cat."

"She's a good cat, but she's deaf. Lots of white cats are deaf."

114

"I didn't know that. Why is that?"

"Something about genes, I don't know. My daughter could tell you. She goes to college. You're one of the kids down to the camp, aren't you?"

"Yes." He looked at some boxes of raspberries and felt in his pocket. He never had spent the five dollars his mother had given him when she took off. Every time he tried to, Stevie or Alex would tell him to hang on to it. "How much are the raspberries?"

"One-fifty a box." At Eddie's expression, he said, "Always expensive this early in the season."

"I'll take two boxes." They weren't very big boxes, but there would be a few for everybody. Fawn was crazy about raspberries.

As he paid the man, he said, "You ever need anybody to tend the stand?"

"Well, no, I don't, 'cause my wife and kids fill in when I'm busy. Maybe later in the summer I'll need somebody to do some weeding. Where you from?"

"New York."

The man smiled. "Do you know a weed from a cabbage?"

"No, sir, but I think a cabbage might be bigger. Anyway, I learn quick."

"If I need anybody, I'll keep you in mind. What's your name?"

"Edward Sanders."

The man gave him his change with his left hand and stuck out his right to shake hands. "I'm Ezra Mason. Pleased to meet you."

Eddie walked on up the road carrying his raspberries

carefully and whistling. That seemed like a nice man, Ezra Mason, even if he was just drumming up trade. And maybe he meant it about a job.

He came to Mrs. Haines's house and stopped to look at it. She was at the post office, so he felt free to stare. It was a white clapboard house set back from the road with a neat lawn in front edged with bushes. It was quite a big house, but he knew Mrs. Haines and her husband had had four boys, all of them now living so far off she almost never got to see her grandchildren.

He liked Mrs. Haines a whole lot, and today they were going fishing at four o'clock. She had called her friend at the highway patrol, and he was calling around the state to see if there had been any word from Alaska. So far, no luck. Eddie had two minds about Stevie's father. He knew she'd worry till she got in touch with him, but when she did find him, then what? He didn't believe for one minute that Mr. Martin was going to say, "Stevie, you come on up to Alaska and bring those two Sanders kids with you," or "Your uncle Tim is just dying to have you bring those Brooklyn kids to his cow farm." No way was that going to happen. If Stevie went (and he could hardly bear to think of it), maybe he and Fawn could stay with Alex a little while longer, but then what? Alex didn't want to get stuck with two kids he didn't even know. He'd come up here, he'd said when they first met him, because he wanted to be alone.

Eddie sighed. No point in spoiling his good raspberry mood with a lot of what-ifs. He wondered who mowed Mrs. Haines's grass. Maybe he could get a job mowing lawns. He'd never touched a lawn mower in his life, but he could learn. If Stevie could drive a tractor, he could run a lawn mower. He'd ask Mrs. Haines.

He turned around and walked back to meet Stevie and Fawn at the dock. He'd finished reading *The Velveteen Rabbit* to Fawn for about the tenth time. He wondered what she'd bring home this time. She liked to hear her favorites over and over.

The girls were not at the town dock, but old Mr. Gavin, who owned the grocery store, was loading boxes of groceries into his big motorboat. Mr. Gavin had turned the running of the store over to his son, and he usually sat on a kitchen chair tipped back against the storefront, smoking a pipe and watching people go by.

He looked up as Eddie came out on the dock. "Afternoon, son." He was breathing hard. "I know summer's here when I have to get the old ark out and start deliverin' groceries to the summer folks."

"How often do you do that?" Eddie asked.

"Twice a week. Used to take it four times a week to that camp where you fellas are stayin'. Back when they had a campful of boys. I remember that young fella you're staying with, though he's grown a whole lot. But that's what the young ones do, they grow up."

"I hope so," Eddie said. "I haven't grown a quarter of an inch in six months."

"Be patient." The old man leaned against the box he was trying to hoist into the boat. "The stuff folks buy gets heavier and heavier."

"I'll get it." Eddie got his arms around the big box and

lifted it into the boat. Mr. Gavin was too old to be doing this; what was his son thinking of? "I can get the rest of them for you." He began carefully loading the remaining boxes into the boat, remembering what Alex was always telling him about balance. "If I get it wrong, you tell me," he said. Maybe Mr. Gavin arranged them in the order of the cottages he stopped at.

Mr. Gavin sat down on the upturned rowboat that lay on the dock. "You're doin' a good job." He was still breathing hard. When Eddie had finished, he said, "I thank you, young fella. I don't know a kid in this town would offer and do a thing like that." He pulled his wallet out of his hip pocket and began to take out a bill.

"No, don't pay me," Eddie said. "You didn't hire me to do it. I just felt like doing it. But Mr. Gavin, if you ever need a box boy or anybody to load the boat regular, anything like that, I'm looking for a job."

"How old are you, son?"

"Fourteen," Eddie said, crossing his fingers.

The old man winked. "And I'm thirty-nine. But that's all right. I like spunk. If I was running the store, I'd hire you tomorrow, but I ain't got much say there anymore. But I thank you for your kindness." He untied the worn rope, threw it into the bow, and stepped in as Eddie steadied the boat for him. He started the old motor, it died, and he started it again. It coughed and then roared. The breeze made his thin white hair stand up straight. He gave Eddie a smart salute and backed the boat away from the dock and down the lake.

I made two friends, Eddie thought, watching the boat

head out into the lake, its stern low in the water. Or, anyway, two guys who will talk to me. He picked up the bag with the boxes of raspberries and put them carefully under the bow seat in their own boat.

The girls were coming down the street with armfuls of books. Dark clouds were piling up in the east.

"Mrs. Haines sent you a message," Stevie said when she reached the dock. "The radio says thundershowers. She says if it's okay with you, she'll postpone fishing till day after tomorrow, same time"—she smiled at him—"same station. Why are you looking so pleased with yourself?"

"I had two conversations and I bought some raspberries."

"Raspberries!" Fawn shrieked. "Eddie!"

Thunder rumbled somewhere far away.

Alex came running down the road from the Terry place. "Wait for me." He caught up with them. "Can't work in the rain, and I'm not about to paddle the old canoe home in a thunderstorm. All aboard, crew."

They got to camp just ahead of the rain.

Chapter 17

ALEX BUILT A FIRE IN THE FIREPLACE WITH SOME OF
the kindling and split logs that he and Eddie had brought
down to the rec building. It had been hard for Eddie to
believe, as he sweated and beat off the mosquitoes in the
clearing in the woods, that they would ever need a fire,
but now he was glad they could have one. It was raining
hard, and the air was chilly.

Stevie opened cans of roast beef hash and heated them
up on the tiny stove. When the fire in the fireplace died
down a little, she moved the frying pan to the open fire
to heat it faster.

"My sister sent me a check today," Alex said. "Tomorrow I'm going to take you guys out for a real meal.
What do you say?"

"When I'm a grown-up," Fawn said, "I'll send *you* a
check, Eddie."

Eddie laughed. "I'll send you one, too, Fawnsel. We'll
flood the mails with money."

While they were eating, Eddie said, "That old man Mr.

Gavin ought not to be hoisting those heavy boxes of groceries. He was puffing like an old truck."

"He's always done it," Alex said.

"He's too old now."

"It's all he's got left to do. Young Percy runs everything."

Eddie and Fawn divided the raspberries into four dishes and they ate them sitting on the floor in front of the fireplace. They all ducked as lightning hit somewhere close by with a nearly simultaneous crash of thunder.

Alex got up and lighted one of the Coleman lanterns. "Glad we got home ahead of that." They could hear the hard slap of the waves against the dock. "We'd better let down the shutters."

He and Eddie ran outside in the rain and unhooked the heavy shutters that fitted over the windows. The rain was already pouring in on the floor. Stevie moved the folding chairs out of the wet area.

With the windows shuttered, the hall was dark. When he came in, Alex lit the other lantern, and they sat closer to the fire. The light from outside that filtered in through the two small glassed windows on the forest side looked eerie.

"I'd better see if the boat's all right." Alex grabbed his nylon windbreaker and ran outside.

Suddenly Eddie jumped up. "The mezuzah. It'll blow away."

Stevie called to him to put on a sweater, but he was already racing down the path to the tent. When he came back, he brought the Grinnell sweatshirt with him. Water was streaming off his dark hair. "I put it inside." He pulled off his soaked T-shirt and put on the sweatshirt.

"I thought you were going to get killed by lightning," Fawn said.

"Not me. I can run faster than lightning." He gave Fawn his last two raspberries and pulled her close to him. She was shaking. "Hey, I didn't mean to scare you."

"Tomorrow I'm going to give you a haircut, Eddie," Alex said. "You look like an Indian brave."

"Do you know how?"

"Sure. I always used to cut Jerome's hair when he lived at home. He was terrified of barbers."

"Who is Jerome?" Fawn said.

"My brother." He pulled a postcard out of his jeans pocket and showed it to them. His name and address had obviously been written by someone else, but in the message space in big block letters, it said ALEX. MISS YOU. XXXXX. "He must be feeling a little happier," he said. "To think about me and write."

"Is he a little boy?" Fawn asked. "My age?"

"No." Alex sounded sad. "He's twenty-one, but in his head he's a little boy."

Lightning lit up the hall and thunder crashed. It seemed so close, Alex jumped up to make sure it hadn't hit the building. Almost at once there was an earsplitting crack, and hail pounded the roof. Fawn cried out and threw her arms around Eddie.

Alex opened the door a few inches and looked out, getting a faceful of rain and hail. He shut the door quickly.

"Looks like it hit the top of the flagpole," he said. "But that's okay."

Stevie looked at Fawn's white face. "Have you got your radio broadcaster here?" she said to Eddie.

"No, it's in the tent, but I can fake it. Listen, Fawn, there's a broadcast coming up."

She looked up at him. "A good one?"

"Real good." He cleared his throat, and using his radio voice, he spoke above the noise of the storm. "This is your FM Station WET, and it's time for Story Hour, so get comfy and prepare for thrills and chills and happy endings. This is your old uncle Eddie Everready with today's story." Thunder crashed. He held Fawn tighter and raised his voice. "Today's story is about two little kids named Hunsel and Gunsel. Are you ready?"

"Yes!" Fawn said.

"Now Hunsel and Gunsel had very mean parents, and those mean parents turned the children out of the house one day right in the middle of a thunderstorm, and they said, 'Get lost, kids.' Well, naturally Hunsel and Gunsel felt terrible. They knew if they went off into the woods, they'd never find their way back. But Gunsel had an idea. She grabbed a box of spaetzle from the kitchen and stuck it under her T-shirt, and as they went down the dark path into the woods with thunder crashing all around them, she kept dropping little pieces of spaetzle. It was the dried kind that you add water to to make delicious dumplings. 'We can follow that trail back home, get it?' Gunny said to her brother. 'When maybe the parents will have changed their minds and they'll be crying 'cause they miss us.' 'Got it,' Hunsel said. 'Very good thinking.'

"But a little later, Hunny said to Gunny, 'Sis,' he said, 'I hate to break this to you, but the rain is turning the spaetzle into dumplings, and the sea gulls are eating them.'

"Gunny felt terrible, but they had to keep going because now they didn't know how to get back. It rained harder and harder." Eddie waited a minute for a new roll of thunder to die away. "But guess what happened?"

"What?" Fawn said anxiously.

"Right in the middle of the forest they came to this beautiful cheesecake house with a strawberry roof. And it was waterproof! Don't ask me how it got waterproofed because I wasn't there, but I think it was magic. Anyway they were very happy and they went in. 'Oi vey! The luck of the Irish!' cried Hunny. All the furniture was made of chocolate. Doorknobs, lamps, chairs, and tables, all chocolate, and a great big bed of marzipan. Man, were they happy! They took off their wet shoes so's not to mess up the graham-cracker-crust floor and right away they ate the bird cage. Don't worry, there wasn't any bird. The bird cage was made of toasted marshmallows."

Rain dripping down the chimney made the logs sizzle. Alex reached out and put another log on the fire.

"Now, children," Eddie said, "you think there's going to be a witch in this story. Well, you're right. There was a big, awkward witch named Bubble, and she had plans to catch the children in the bird cage and eat them for dinner. But where was the bird cage?"

"Gone!" Fawn said.

"Gone! So the witch started to chase the children. She chased them right out into the storm, and at that very moment—"

As if on cue thunder crashed, and the hail beat down even more heavily.

"Right then a fireball hit the witch on the top of her pointed cap, rolled right down her skinny side to her feet, and pitched her into the lake. I forgot to mention the lake. And the witch hit the water with a big sizzle and disappeared and there was nothing left but a little sprinkle of ashes on the water. So Hunsel and Gunsel lived happily ever after in the cheesecake house, growing taller and slightly fatter from all that chocolate, playing checkers with M&M's, and having a ball. That's all for today, children, from your old spinner of lies, Uncle Eddie the Everready. See you tomorrow. Stay tuned." Pretending exhaustion, Eddie rolled over on his back with his arms outstretched.

"Bravo!" Alex said.

"You've driven away the storm," Stevie said.

The hail had changed to the softer sound of rain, and the thunder was moving off into the distance.

When Fawn was in bed, Eddie read her a chapter from an old book the librarian had found for her, *Hans Brinker and the Silver Skates*.

"Maybe the lake will turn to ice overnight," Fawn murmured sleepily, "and we can go skating."

Alex and Stevie were drinking coffee and staring into the fire. Eddie looked at them. "Well," he said as casually as he could, "I guess I'll hit the sack. In my tent."

125

"Do you want us to move?" Stevie said. "We're in your way." She touched the cot Eddie usually slept on.

"No, no. I'm going to sleep in my tent. You girls can get along without my protection by now, right?"

Stevie laughed. "We'll try, Ed. See you in the morning."

Eddie went out the door and ran down the dark path, the rain blowing in his face.

In his mind he said, EDDX3 to GRAM7. Keep an eye on those bears, will ya? Over to you.

GRAM7 to EDDX3. Not to worry. Over and out.

Chapter 16

THE TENT WAS DRY. EDDIE KEPT THE SIDES ROLLED down all the time, unlike Alex, who had kept his up until the rainstorm today. Eddie pulled his cot into the middle of the tent. He had forgotten to bring the blanket, but he could put on all his T-shirts and wrap the Grinnell sweatshirt around his legs. It wasn't really cold, just cool after all the hot days they'd had.

He went around the tent with his flashlight, inspecting it carefully to make sure no squirrels or chipmunks or snakes had managed to get in. On a night like this, they ought to be in their dens or whatever they lived in. He tied the front flap of the tent securely and got into bed with the flashlight still on.

I didn't brush my teeth, he thought. Gram wouldn't like that. Gram was big on toothbrushing. But she wouldn't want him to go out in the rain and get soaked, and there wasn't any water in the tent. He'd brush them twice in the morning.

He wished he had a pillow. There wasn't a single pillow in the whole camp. They ought to get some kind of medal for survival under conditions of extreme hardship, if they ever got out of here.

He wished he had the real Walkman Gram had given him. His mother had grabbed it, like everything else. Alex kept his radio up at the rec building so they could all hear it. Alex was very thoughtful that way. But he, Edward Sanders, he decided, was not thoughtful. Unthoughtful Eddie, Eddie the Unthoughtful. He aimed the flashlight at the back of the tent. Had there been a noise back there?

He was glad Fawn could sleep up at the rec building without him. If he wasn't kidding himself, he'd have to admit she probably could have all along. She didn't hang on him all the time anymore. To tell the truth, he missed it. Maybe it's me that wants to hang on to her, he thought.

He hadn't told anybody, but he would be thirteen this week. Fawn might remember, but probably not. She probably didn't even know what month it was.

With his fingers he spread his long wet hair out over the edge of the cot. He hoped Alex really knew how to cut hair. It would be awful to look like a freak. He thought of Alex's brother. That must be rough. What if Fawn had been handicapped in any way? He shuddered.

He was almost asleep, with the flashlight still on, when he heard a far-off scream. He sat bolt upright. It came again. He relaxed. It was that crazy loon bird. He'd heard it before. It really did sound like a woman screaming. Alex said they carried their babies on their backs.

"Get in out of the rain, loony," he said aloud. "Put your babies to bed."

He lay down again, and this time he turned out the flashlight. At first the darkness seemed so thick, he didn't think he could stand it. But he wouldn't let himself turn on the light. It would wear out the battery if he left it on. Anyway, Alex would see it and think he was scared of the dark.

"Not me," he said aloud. "Not me, Edward Sanders, the fearless Knight of the North Woods." He made himself relax. It took some time, but at last he went to sleep.

When he woke, it was early morning. Faint light filtered into the tent, and he heard birds back in the woods making their sleepy waking-up sounds. He had never heard them so clearly from the rec building. It sounded cool.

The rain had stopped, but when he opened the front flap of the tent, he saw that the sky was still heavy with gray clouds. Maybe more rain later.

He got his toothbrush and toothpaste and a towel and went down to the edge of the lake. He hoped he wasn't polluting the lake with toothpaste. He also hoped the lake water wasn't polluting him. He was careful not to swallow any. He splashed the cold water on his face and thought about going in for a short swim. But then he remembered the camp rule about not swimming alone. He wasn't really all that good a swimmer yet, but he could keep himself afloat and moving. Alex said he had to learn not to fling his arms around so much.

The camp was quiet. He didn't want to go to the toilet

in the rec building when they were still asleep. He guessed it would be okay to go back into the woods, if he went far enough.

Until now he had been no further into the woods than the woodpile, and that was hardly any way at all. Alex said there was a footpath that went all around the lake. Maybe if he walked in as far as the path and just a little beyond . . . He stood looking at the forest. Even when the sun was out, it looked dark in there. In the stories Gram used to read him, like the Grimms and Hans Christian Andersen, there always seemed to be a dark forest that was scary.

Well, stupid, he said to himself, that's the way the world is. What do you expect—interstates? Shopping malls?

He definitely had to go. He walked around the back of his tent and climbed the slope that led into the woods. The dry brown pine needles under his feet made him slip. He needed Hans Brinker's silver skates.

He was in the trees now, tall white pines with branches loaded with soft-looking needles, and pitch pines with branches starting high up the trunk. Alex had told him the difference. Once you knew, it was easy to tell. Like beauty and the beast, the white pines were pretty and well-balanced, while the pitch pines grew all crooked and twisted, like trees in a nightmare. Underfoot now he was stepping in ferns and small bushes. He took small gingerly steps, keeping a watchful eye out for snakes. Alex insisted that the only dangerous snakes in these parts were rattlesnakes, and they were usually found much farther back in the woods near rock piles.

But *usually* didn't mean always. And dangerous or not, he didn't want his foot coming down on some wriggly snake.

He came to the path and crossed it. The birds were quieting down now, as the day lightened. He stood still and listened. It was surprising how many sounds there were in here. He'd always thought the forest was silent. But it was full of little sounds that you wouldn't hear if you didn't listen carefully.

He jumped as a chipmunk chittered at him and ran up a pine, swinging out on a branch and watching him with bright eyes. He'd learned to like chipmunks. Fawn had gotten one to eat out of her hand.

"Good morning," he said. "I'm going to use your house for a bathroom, and that's really crude, isn't it? I'm sorry." He went a few steps beyond the chipmunk's tree and unzipped his shorts.

When you got clear into the woods, it didn't seem as dark as it did from outside. The trees and ferns and things smelled wonderful after the rain. He decided to go a little farther. He wished he had his switchblade to make small nicks on the trees he passed, like they did in explorer stories, so he could find his way back. That's what old Gunsel should have done, her and her spaetzle. He began to feel like Daniel Boone.

A sudden weird grunt stopped him. He looked wildly around. Rattlesnakes didn't grunt, and bears didn't hang out in trees. This sound came from a tree. After a minute he found it: a toad, gray and mottled, with enormous bulging eyes, staring at him from a tree directly in front of him.

He relaxed. "You are the ugliest thing I ever saw," he said. "If you don't mind my saying so." The toad or frog or whatever it was looked as if it were grinning. "All right, so you think I'm ugly, too. It's a tie." He walked carefully around the tree, in case the toad should take it into its head to jump at him.

A squirrel leaped out of his way. He would go back in a minute. He didn't want to get lost in here, but it was definitely an interesting place. He'd had no idea.

He found some tiny pink flowers growing in a swampy place. He started to pick them for Fawn, but then he didn't because they looked so nice where they were. Maybe he could bring her in here some morning and show her.

The wind had blown down some branches. They'd make good kindling; he picked up a few, but in a minute he got tired of carrying them because they kept bumping into the trees. He could always come back and get a load later.

"You're turning into a pretty good woodsman, Edward," he told himself, "even to think of it. If you were strolling down Forty-second Street and you saw a bunch of pine boughs, you wouldn't tell yourself to take them home. In fact, you'd think you were on coke or something."

He took a deep breath of the fresh, piney air. He stepped across a brook, into a small grove of young birch trees, slender and graceful like girls in white dresses. He ran his hand lightly over the smooth bark. He wished he had brought Fawn with him. Well, maybe tomorrow.

Suddenly a cloud of midges flew into his face, getting into his eyes and nose. He opened his mouth to say, "Hey!" and got some in his mouth. Batting at them with both hands, he scooped water out of the shallow brook to splash his face and neck and arms. Once he jumped back across the brook, they disappeared as quickly as they had come. But half a dozen black flies had discovered him. They buzzed around his head, and one bit him on the neck.

Well, nothing was perfect. He walked fast for a minute, slapping at the flies. Alex used some kind of antibug stuff when he went for a walk in the woods. Now Eddie could see why he bothered.

Suddenly he had the feeling that he was going in a circle, and he began to feel panicky. The old fairy stories were right: The forest was an easy place to get lost. Trees looked alike.

He made himself stand still to think. What things had he noticed when he came along here? *If* he did come along here. He listened for the brook and couldn't hear it. "Be still," he said to some bird that was making a noise like a hammer. But the rat-a-tat kept up, and he moved so he could see who was making all the racket. It was a bird about ten or eleven inches long with a bright red head, shiny black feathers, white tail feathers, and a white breast. It was pounding away at the trunk of a pine like a jackhammer. Eddie was fascinated. The bird must be nuts; he'd fracture his stupid skull or at least get a humongous headache. But he or she certainly was pretty. Eddie was so interested, he forgot for a moment that he was lost. A woodpecker. It had to be a woodpecker. He'd heard of them, but he hadn't realized they really went at it like that.

The woodpecker stopped for a moment, and Eddie heard the faint murmur of the brook. He made his way through the brush to the stream, and after a minute of searching, he saw his footprint in the muddy edge of the water.

"Piece of cake," he said.

He was almost back to the path that ran around the lake when something slithered out of the brush in front of him. He yelled and jumped backward. The snake paused and half turned toward him, darting its tongue in and out of its mouth. Eddie stood frozen. You *know* it's not a rattlesnake, he told himself. You know it. Rattlesnakes are bigger and thicker and they have diamonds on their backs. Alex had shown him pictures of different kinds of snakes. He said only the rattlers were dangerous. It was a garter snake, this one was. Harmless. They didn't bite, but he wished it wouldn't keep sticking its tongue in and out like that, fast as lightning.

Then the snake was gone, moving so quickly Eddie hardly saw it disappear into the tall ferns. He felt ashamed of himself for being so scared. The snake lived here; this was its space.

"Sorry, snake," he said. "Didn't mean to bust into your territory. Have a nice day."

A few minutes later he was back in his tent. "Gram," he said aloud, "the world is full of surprises."

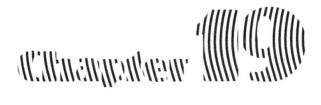

Chapter 19

EDDIE BEGAN TO FEEL NERVOUS AS HE SAW ALEX SET-
ting up one of the folding chairs outside on the pine needles
and laying out a pair of shears and clippers and a comb
on a stump beside it.

"Maybe we could do it some other day," Eddie said.

Alex grinned. "Chicken."

Fawn settled down on the ground to watch, her thin
arms wrapped around her knees. "Eddie, you do need a
haircut. You look like that girl in the story that let her
hair down for somebody to climb up it."

Stevie laughed. "Rapunzel."

"She was a blond," Eddie said.

"Ready for the customer." Alex waved a towel at Eddie.

"But is the customer ready for you?" Reluctantly Eddie
sat, and Alex put the towel around his neck and tied the
ends.

"I can't see what you're doing," Eddie said. "Barbers
have mirrors."

Stevie ran inside and came back with the small shaving

mirror that hung on a nail in the bathroom. "Now you can watch every move."

Alex made an elaborate gesture with the scissors over Eddie's head. "A magic act is about to take place. This young man whom you have all mistaken for an escapee from the age of hippies is about to turn into the all-American boy."

"The all-American schlemiel," Eddie muttered. He closed his eyes as Alex made the first cut and a long lock of hair fell onto the pine needles. "Ever since I met you guys, I'm always putting myself in your hands. It's dangerous."

Stevie brought out Alex's cassette player and put in a Joan Armatrading tape. Eddie's feet tapped to the rhythm.

"Sit still," Alex said, "or I'll cut your ear off. By mistake, of course."

Snip snip snip. Dark hair piled up around the chair. Stevie got the broom and swept it into the wooden crate they used for a trash can.

A man in an old boat rowed slowly along the shore, watching them. Alex waved to him, and the man waved back and rowed toward them.

"I've seen that guy hanging around here before," Eddie said.

"Shh. Voices carry over the water. It's the minister."

"Nice morning," the minister said a minute later, as his boat grazed the dock.

"Little mite cloudy."

Eddie smiled to himself. When Alex talked to these people, he sounded like them. He wondered if he did it on purpose or just picked it up, the way Eddie knew he had sounded more Jewish when he was around Gram.

"You're a good barber."

"Thanks. Would you like to come ashore? Have a cup of coffee?"

"No, no, thank you kindly. Just out enjoying a little exercise. I'm Reverend Fuller. Wanted to welcome you to our little community and urge you to come to our church at any time you can."

Politely Alex said, "Thank you. We're kind of a motley crew. Stephanie here is a Lutheran, my folks are Greek Orthodox, and Eddie and Fawn are half-Jewish, half-Irish."

"My goodness," the minister said. "That really is ecumenical, isn't it. Well, you're all welcome. Some of my congregation are very curious about you."

But not you, buster, Eddie said to himself. Oh no, not you. You're just snooping around here for the exercise, to build up those deltoids. Reverend What's-his-name was taking it all in, the rec building, the rebuilt dock, the canoe lying on the shore, the old outboard, the kids.

"Well, nice meeting you all." The man pushed away from the dock and went on along the shoreline—where he could take a good look at the cove and the tents. Eddie wanted to call after him, "We had to cut down the marijuana trees; they were making too much shade." Instead he muttered, "Nosy," and bent his head as Alex trimmed the back.

"Don't be so intolerant," Alex said. "It's natural for them to wonder about us. We're an odd quartet."

"I never met a reverend, a priest, or a rabbi that I didn't feel spied on," Eddie said.

"You're paranoid," Alex said. "Tip your head a little. That's it."

"How can I see what you're doing when you've got my head hanging on my chest?"

"You look beautiful, Eddie," Fawn said.

Stevie put in a new tape, the Kinks, and turned it up a little louder. Eddie wanted to look at her and grin because he knew she was reacting to the reverend the way he had, only showing it in her own way. But Alex was running the clippers along the back of his neck, so he couldn't move. Good old Stevie; he was getting so he could often tell what she was thinking, even though she was quiet, and it was often much the same thing he was thinking.

"Ladies and gentlemen," Alex said, "behold before your very eyes, Edward Sanders, junior yuppie." With a dramatic gesture he swept the towel off.

Eddie grabbed up the mirror and looked at himself. "Oi vey! I'm a skinhead!" He clapped his hand to the short curly hair that fit his head now like a cap. "I feel like a whisk broom."

"You look great," Stevie said. "Really, Eddie."

As the Kinks cut loose, Eddie leaped out of his chair and began break dancing on the dock. Fawn joined him. Eddie flung out his arms, leaped, did a handstand, and shouted, "It's the New Me!"

A little way past the cove the Reverend Fuller shipped his oars and looked on in amazement.

 Chapter 20

A HARD RAIN THE NEXT DAY SPOILED EDDIE'S AND MRS. Haines's fishing plans, but shortly after five o'clock Tom Terry brought her in his outboard. She climbed out of Tom's boat before anyone could help her, bundled up in a yellow oilskin coat and a matching wide-brimmed hat, waving a package.

"Mail from Alaska!" she shouted. Clutching it under her coat to keep it dry, she hurried up the path to the rec house, where they all crowded out on the steps to greet her, Stevie running down the path.

"She was going to *row* over here in this downpour," Tom Terry said, when he had tied up the boat and joined them inside, rain pouring off him in puddles at his feet. "Crazy woman doesn't have a motorboat since her old one gave out."

"The mail must go through," Mrs. Haines said, with a dramatic flourish. "Neither rain nor snow nor broken motors . . ."

They were all trying not to watch Stevie, who had gone off to a corner of the stage to read the bulky letter that had come by express mail. Eddie kept glancing at her anxiously out of the corner of his eye.

Alex had a fire going in the fireplace, and now he added more wood and began to make coffee.

"Sunday is the Fourth of July, in case you hadn't noticed," Mrs. Haines said. "I'm inviting you to my house for dinner. You camp people and you, Tom, Annette, and that nice librarian. And I thought I might ask Joe McCord. He's the one who's been trying to find out if Stevie's father put out a missing bulletin. I'll have to call him tonight and tell him she's heard."

"Myra," Tom said, teasing her, "are you trying to fix up a romance between the librarian and Joe McCord?"

"No, I am not," she said. Then she added, "But neither of them could do better. Joe is a sweetheart, and he needs a nice wife like Diana. Alex, this coffee would walk on its own two feet!"

"I could add some hot water. The milk's all gone."

"No, no, I wasn't complaining. I like coffee that tastes like coffee." She looked around. "You're very nice and snug in here. Not even a leak in the roof."

"Stevie reshingled."

They all looked up as Stevie jumped down off the stage and came toward them, carrying several sheets of paper. Her face was hard to read. She sat down on the stump near the fire.

"Well," she said. "At least we're in contact, and that's the main thing."

140

"I 'spose he told you how to find your uncle," Eddie said. He was trying hard not to look depressed. I ought to feel happy that Stevie doesn't have to worry anymore, he thought.

She looked around at them. "Some of it's kind of hard to tell, but you're like my family now."

"Listen," Alex said, "you don't have to tell us anything."

"I want to." She took a deep breath. "The chamber of commerce finally found him. He's not in Valdez; he's in a town about ten miles from there. Anyway, the same day he got my letter, he got back the letter and check he'd sent to me in care of Uncle Tim, and a short letter from my . . . uh . . . aunt. I'll read you that one." She shook out the paper.

"Dear Joseph:

I don't know what kind of games you're playing. First you have the nerve to ask us to take on your child, when I don't even know you. Then my husband, who is not well, drives all the way to Boston in all that traffic, and no kid shows up. If this is some kind of joke, I don't appreciate it. You have upset Timothy to where he's almost had a heart attack. To be honest with you, if we don't hear from you ever again, it will be too soon.

Yours truly,
Eunice W. Martin."

Tom Terry let out a low whistle.

"There's nothing like family feeling," Alex said. "She and my father would get along great."

Eddie suddenly laughed. "What if Eunice W. Martin had found all three of us!"

Impulsively Mrs. Haines put her hand on Eddie's arm. "Well, it's her loss," she said. "Now, Stevie, what does your father say to all this?"

"Well, he's furious with Uncle Tim, or mostly with his wife. He says Tim was a good kid, but he never had a lot of spunk and obviously he married a witch. He says thank God six or eight times that we missed connections with Uncle Tim." She paused. "He's kind of worried about our . . . uh . . . arrangement, I think he calls it."

"Perfectly natural," Mrs. Haines said. "He probably pictures Alex as some kind of pot-smoking, girl-chasing teenager. If you don't object, Stevie, I'll write to him and try to reassure him. You might do that, too, Tom, you and Annette."

"He wants me to phone him," Stevie said. "He doesn't have a phone himself, but there's one in his boardinghouse, and he said if I could call on the Fourth of July, he'd be off work and he'd just hang around the phone all day. There's the time difference. He suggests around six o'clock our time."

"That will work out fine. You'll all be at my house for dinner." Mrs. Haines explained to Stevie about her invitation. "And we can all talk to him. Joe McCord, too; he can add the force of the law."

Eddie said, "Did he say anything about us?"

"Only surprise to hear you're with us. No comment one way or the other. I think he had too much else on his mind. He's met you, he knows you're nice kids."

142

"Stevie, he doesn't know that. All we ever said to each other was hello. He probably thinks we're a couple of freeloaders, sponging off you and Alex."

"Eddie, don't say dumb things. My father trusts my judgment more than that. Don't forget, I took my mother's place and ran the house for three years."

"What does he say about the end of the summer? That is, if you stay here till then. Then what?"

Stevie hesitated. "He said I could come to Alaska, but I can tell he isn't too thrilled about that. He likes the way he's living. I think he's more, like, carefree than he's ever been. He runs a forklift on the dock, and he likes it."

"Well, don't worry about the end of summer now," Mrs. Haines said. "It's only the second of July. Tom, we'd better get started, before that lake roughs up any more. See you Sunday, all." To Eddie she said, "On Monday at five o'clock you and I go fishing, come hell or high water."

She had her hand on his shoulder, and he wanted very much to hug her and tell her he was scared about what would become of Fawn and him. But he grinned at her and said, "Do I have to put the worm on the hook?"

"I'll do it the first time," she whispered. She gave him a little hug. "Not to worry." She leaned down and kissed Fawn on the cheek. "Take good care of Eddie."

"I will," Fawn said. "Watch this." She stood on her hands and then did a cartwheel.

"Wonderful! I spent years trying to do a cartwheel and I never could."

"I'll teach you," Fawn said.

They watched Tom Terry and the broad yellow-clad

figure of Mrs. Haines get into the boat, wave good-bye, and putt-putt off toward town.

"I love Mrs. Haines," Stevie said, "and the Terrys, too."

Mrs. Haines's warmth had erased Eddie's fears—at least for the moment. He held the palm of his hand in front of his mouth. "Ladies and gentlemen, this broadcast is coming to you from Crystal Lake Camp, where all the chipmunks are friendly, all the fish are fantastic, and all the humans are hungry. The next sound you hear will be teeth crunching down on peanut-butter sandwiches. Stay tuned."

Chapter 21

Eddie hung around Gavins' store until he saw Mr. Gavin Junior come out of his tiny office at the back, wearing his white overalls and the bookkeeper's eyeshade.

"Excuse me, Mr. Gavin," he said.

"Yes?" Mr. Gavin Junior was about fifty, sandy-haired, thin, lacking the sharp intelligence of his father.

"I was wondering if you'd like to hire a box boy for Saturdays."

"Box boy?" Mr. Gavin shoved his steel-rimmed glasses up on his nose. "What do I want with a box boy?"

"Well, I've noticed that most of your summer people shop on Saturdays, and I suppose they're mostly city people and they're used to having some boy carry their groceries out to their cars. I thought it might improve your business."

Eddie waited patiently. He could see that Mr. Gavin the Younger was not a quick man with a new idea.

"They have to shop here whether they get their goods

carried out or not," he said finally. "Where else they going to go?"

"Some of them go to Gorham," Eddie said, not knowing whether they did or not. "Some go to Berlin."

Mr. Gavin scowled.

"They are used to having their groceries carried out and I got a hunch they hate to do it themselves," Eddie said soothingly, as if comforting Mr. Gavin for his bad luck.

Mr. Gavin studied Eddie and said, "Ain't you that kid that helped my father load his boat?"

"I did help him one day, yes, sir."

"And I suppose you think I owe you."

"Sir, I didn't mention it. You did."

The senior clerk, who had been listening with amusement as he sprinkled the fresh vegetables, said, "He's got you there, Perc." The man was small and bent over, almost as old as the elder Mr. Gavin. "Whyn't you give him a crack at it?"

"How much pay do you expect?" Mr. Gavin said.

"Minimum wage," Eddie said promptly.

Mr. Gavin hooted. "One dollar an hour, take it or leave it."

"Two dollars," Eddie said.

"One fifty."

"One seventy-five."

"There's a law against child labor."

"Oh, come off it, Perc," the clerk said. "Who cares? Take him."

Eddie knew why the clerk was on his side. The man

146

was stiff with arthritis, and sometimes he got stuck with carrying out heavy bags.

Mr. Gavin sniffed and blew his nose. "Be here Saturday at nine A.M. on the dot. We'll try it for one day. One day only, mind you. No promises."

"Yes sir. I'll be here. Thank you very much." Eddie walked with dignity out of the store, but as soon as he hit the sidewalk he broke into a run.

He burst into the post office just as Mrs. Haines was closing for the weekend. Fawn was there waiting for him. "I got it! I got the job! Next Saturday, nine A.M."

"Eddie, that's terrific!" Mrs. Haines clapped her hands, and her blue eyes shone with delight. "Keep careful track of your time. Don't let Perc Gavin cheat you."

"He said we'd try it for one day only, but if I can get in there once, I can keep it. I'll work my tail off." He swung Fawn off her feet. "I'm a workin' man!"

"Speaking of that," Mrs. Haines said, "how about mowing my lawn this afternoon? I've got you all coming to dinner tomorrow and my lawn looks like a hay field."

"I'll help," Fawn said.

"While Eddie mows the grass, you and I will wash celery and peel potatoes and slice onions. I'm going to have salmon, because that's what my husband and the boys and I always had for Fourth of July dinner." For a moment she looked over their heads, as if she had forgotten them.

"Do you catch the salmon?" Fawn asked.

"No." Myra Haines smiled. "It's Atlantic salmon, caught out in the ocean. They're getting scarce, those lovely big pink ones, but there are still some. And I make an egg sauce with capers that's the best thing you ever put in your mouth."

"Where's Stevie?" Eddie said.

"She's helping Annette make blueberry pies. Annette always brings the dessert. Alex and Tom are working on a boat. Let's go home and get some lunch before I fall over from hunger." She rolled down the partition between the front of the post office and the area behind the counter and locked everything up. "Well, Eddie," she said, "a real job. That's your declaration of independence."

As they came out of the post office and started up the street, Bubber and three of his friends came barreling down the sidewalk on their bikes. They swerved around Mrs. Haines, but Eddie had to jump out of the way to keep from getting run down. He turned his ankle on the curb and almost fell. The boys' jeering laughter echoed down the street.

A thin woman in clothes too big for her came out of Sandra's Spa. She was scowling, the kind of scowl that doesn't go away.

Mrs. Haines was angry at the boys on the bikes. "Beatrice Perley," she said, "if you don't teach that boy of yours how to behave, he's going to get in real trouble."

Bubber's mother put her hands on her bony hips. "You telling me how to bring up my kids, Myra Haines?"

"Somebody better tell you," Mrs. Haines said, "before it's too late."

Mrs. Perley scornfully looked Eddie and Fawn up and down. "At least he don't hang out with druggies and preverts." She turned her back on them and swung herself insolently up the street.

"Does she mean us?" Eddie said. "Druggies and preverts?" He started to laugh, then stopped. "It would be funny, except I guess she could cause some trouble."

"If she can," Mrs. Haines said, "you can be sure she will."

Chapter 22

If Stevie hadn't been so nervous about calling her father, she would have enjoyed Mrs. Haines's party more. The food was fantastic, and there was an abundance of it, spread out buffet-fashion on the long mahogany dining room table. Potato salad; cold boiled salmon, pink and flaky and not at all like the western salmon she was used to, with Mrs. Haines's secret sauce; hot homemade Parker House rolls; fresh garden peas; a big wooden bowl heaped with fresh lettuce leaves, radishes, sliced cucumbers, and tomatoes. Iced coffee, iced tea, lemonade. And at the end, homemade vanilla ice cream with Mrs. Haines's hot fudge sauce, and blueberry pie.

"You must have stayed up all night cooking," Alex said.

"Oh, Annette did most of it," Mrs. Haines said.

Annette rolled her eyes. "You know better."

"You ought to give up the post office and just feed people," Officer McCord said.

Stevie had been nervous about meeting this man who

had been sending out bulletins about her, but she liked him. Youngish, beginning to go bald, lean and tanned. He told her how glad he was she had heard from her father, and she thanked him for his help. She noticed that Eddie eyed him suspiciously and stayed away from him. Eddie didn't want any cop asking him questions. She was going to make it clear to her father that whatever happened, Eddie and Fawn were going to stay with her. She had told Eddie that, but he looked skeptical. In his opinion, when push came to shove, the grown-ups always won.

He had labored long and hard getting Mrs. Haines's lawn mowed the day before, and now Alex and Tom were setting out a croquet set. Eddie had never seen one.

Stevie went upstairs after they had cleared the dishes away, to go to the bathroom and just to get away from everybody for a minute. The Haines's big three-story white house, built in the nineteenth century, was not at all like Stevie's home in Iowa, which was a one-story ranch-type house, but just being in a comfortable, lived-in house almost overcame her with homesickness.

She wandered down the long corridor on the second floor, looking in at the five bedrooms, all of them different. Mrs. Haines's four sons' rooms were pretty much as they had left them, and it was easy to see the differences in the boys' personalities: the athletic one, with the banners and trophies; the one with the elaborate stereo and racks of tapes and two guitars; the one with a solid wall of books and a brilliant David Hockney poster; the one with pictures of girls. She wished she could meet them sometime.

Mrs. Haines's room was unusually long, probably two

151

rooms with the wall knocked out, and a fireplace at one end. She had a big four-poster bed with a crocheted bedspread, and photographs of her children at all ages were everywhere. The large silver-framed photograph beside the bed would be Mr. Haines.

Stevie wished she could go in and look more closely, but that would be rude. She jumped guiltily a moment later when Mrs. Haines came upstairs.

"I'm being awfully nosy," Stevie said. "Being in a real house is so nice, and it made me think—" She stopped and her eyes filled with tears.

"It made you think of home," Mrs. Haines said. "Come on in." She took her into her own bedroom and sat her down in a yellow chintz chair by the wide windows. "I hope you're here next spring when my apple trees bloom." She pointed to the orchard. "It's like a fairyland. I sit here, where you are, and all I can see is white blossoms."

"My mother had some pear trees she loved."

"What was she like, your mother?"

For a moment Stevie hesitated. How to say what she was like? A light breeze lifted the white lace curtains at the sides of the windows. She could hear the voices of the others out on the lawn playing croquet. She began to tell Mrs. Haines about her mother, the hard work, the laughter, the love of animals and flowers, the closeness they had had together, the books they had read and talked about, the music on the stereo and the Saturday afternoon opera broadcasts, the good food, the neatness.

She stopped. "I didn't mean to give you a whole biography."

"I'm glad you did. It helps me know you better. Stevie, when you call your father, will you let me talk to him for a few minutes?"

"Sure, of course."

"Tom wants to talk to him, too, to make him understand what kind of boy Alex is. I'm sure that could be a worry to your dad. And we'll ring Joe McCord in on the act, too." She smiled. "A little authority never hurts. Because you do see, it's natural for him to worry. We all worry about our children, especially in the teen years. That's when it all breaks loose. I was a heller at sixteen."

Stevie laughed. "I don't believe it."

"You'd better believe it." Mrs. Haines stood up.

"What I worry about most," Stevie said, not wanting her to go yet, "is Eddie and Fawn. I want to keep them with me no matter what."

Mrs. Haines nodded. "I'm on your side. I'd better go tend to my guests now. Stay up here awhile if you feel like being quiet." She looked at her watch. "In about half an hour you can start calling your dad. It may take time to get through on a holiday."

When she had gone, Stevie leaned her head back and closed her eyes. Next to her own mother, Mrs. Haines was the nicest woman she had ever met. How thankful she was that she wasn't at Uncle Tim's, being snarled at by that wife of his.

Stevie held the phone to her ear and listened to the buzzing and ringing. It was the third time she had tried

153

without being able to get an open line. Why did people call each other on the Fourth of July?

It was six-thirty, and she was getting very anxious. What if he thought she wasn't going to call and left the house? She tried to imagine what kind of place an Alaskan boardinghouse would be, full of men who packed fish. Was it noisy? Did they drink a lot?

She was in a small room that had been Mr. Haines's study. It still smelled faintly of pipe tobacco. There was a brass ashtray on the desk, and a German beer mug full of pens and pencils and a ruler. The books on the shelves were mostly legal books, and on the wall there was a framed law school diploma from Columbia, and another certificate saying that Philip Haines had been a member of the New Hampshire legislature.

The others were in the living room. She could hear their voices faintly, and now and then she heard firecrackers from the village. Later there would be fireworks down by the town dock, Mrs. Haines said.

She sat up straight. The phone was ringing in Alaska. Someone said hello.

"Hello?" He said it again impatiently. It was her father.

"Dad." Her voice was so faint, she had to repeat it. "Dad? It's me, Stevie."

"Thank God," he said. "I've been waiting for hours."

"I couldn't get through." She reminded herself that what sounded like annoyance in his voice was worry. He always sounded a little angry when he was worried. "I'm sorry you had to wait. How are you?"

"Well, I'm fine. The question is how are you?"

"Great. Really." She tried to remember the reassuring speech she had rehearsed. She did pretty well, but he kept throwing her off with questions, interrupting her. She hated phones. She wanted to *see* him. She wanted him to see her, how healthy and happy she was. She tried to tell him, but he kept asking questions about the camp, the conditions there, and "this teenager."

"I don't like this teenager arrangement, this boy."

"Dad, you would love Alex. It's too long a story for the phone, but I'll write you all about him, why he's here."

"Where are you? Who's paying for this call? You should have called collect. I told you."

"We're at our friend's, Mrs. Haines. She's the post-mistress. She wants to speak to you." Relieved to get off the phone, she ran to the door and called Mrs. Haines, then waited in the hall, feeling wrung out.

Eddie came out and looked at her. "You okay?"

"Yes, it's just so hard to explain things long-distance."

"Did he say get rid of us?"

"Eddie." She had forgotten how worried he was. "Of course not. He didn't mention you. It's Alex he worries about."

Eddie nodded. "Probably thinks you're having some wild orgy. Well, you can't blame him."

"Well, I do blame him." She felt angry suddenly. "He ought to know me well enough to know I'm not like that."

"Teenagers get weird. I ought to know: I just got to be one."

It took her a minute to hear what he'd said. "What do you mean?"

"You in your ignorance think the nation celebrates the Fourth of July for the Declaration of Independence. No way. It is the birthday of Edward Karl Sanders."

"Eddie! Why didn't you tell us? We'd have had a party. . . ."

"We did."

"Are you kidding?"

"On the level. Today I am a youth."

"What a moment to spring it on me."

"I thought you needed a little distraction."

"I did, I did. Mrs. Haines is talking a long time."

Tom Terry came out into the hall. "I come after Myra. We've got a schedule. Joe comes last, to put the stamp of the law on it."

"Tom, it's Eddie's birthday."

Tom grabbed Eddie's shoulder. "Edward! Come back and tell everybody."

"No, wait till the phoning is over. We've got enough tension floating around here."

It seemed forever before Mrs. Haines came out and motioned Tom to go in. "He's a very nice man," she said. "Very reasonable."

"What did he say?" Stevie was so tense, her stomach hurt.

"I think he's agreeing to your staying where you are for the summer. Later on we'll talk again, about the future, but one thing at a time. He sounded relieved, once he got over being nervous. Of course he's nervous, poor man. I'm glad he didn't hear any sooner from that awful sister-in-law."

When Tom came out, Joe McCord went in. Stevie had no idea what they all were saying to her father, but it seemed to have been the right things, because when she went on to say good-bye to him, he said, "You seem to be in good hands. Thank God for that. They sound like good folks. Now I will send you a check or a money order every two weeks, and I want you to pay your way and bank as much as you can. We'll wait and see what happens later in the summer before we try to make plans for the fall. You can come up here, of course, but I'd have to find a house. It will probably come to that, but we won't worry about that yet. Take care of yourself, listen to Mrs. Haines, take her advice, and be a good girl."

She hung up, after the good-byes, and leaned her head on the desk. She couldn't remember ever feeling so drained.

But in the living room Eddie's birthday was being celebrated with songs, Mrs. Haines playing the piano, and finally a bunch of lighted birthday candles stuck into a piece of blueberry pie. Eddie had a grin that stretched right across his face.

When it grew dark, they went down to the lake to watch the fireworks. By the time that was over, everyone was so tired that Alex spent the night with the Terrys, and Stevie, Fawn, and Eddie slept at Mrs. Haines's house.

As he lay in the comfortable bed that had belonged to the Haineses' youngest son, Eddie stared up at the tiny silver stars that someone had pasted on the ceiling.

"EDDX3 to GRAM7. Do you read me?"

GRAM7 to EDDX3. Loud and clear. Happy birthday! Over.

157

"EDDX3 to GRAM7. Wish you'd been at my party. Over."

GRAM7 to EDDX3. You think I'd miss it? That was me blowing out the candles. You'll get your wish, guaranteed. Over and out.

Chapter 23

MAKING THE CONNECTION WITH STEVIE'S FATHER HAD eased much of the tension that had hung over them all. There was still the question of what would happen in the fall, but for the time being they were trying not to think of it.

Alex was accepted for the autumn term at the boat school in Maine, and it was taken for granted that he would probably come back to work for Tom for at least a while after that. In time he wanted to have a boat yard of his own, but it would take money to set that up, and time to find the best location. Wooden boats were not exactly a hot product, as he reminded them all.

Stevie, acting on Eddie's suggestion, asked Mr. Ezra Mason, at the roadside vegetable stand, if he needed a weeder. When he heard that she had grown up on a farm, he hired her three afternoons a week. Sometimes it was a day that Eddie was working, too, and then Fawn stayed with Annette.

Eddie turned out to be a great help at Gavins' store,

carrying out groceries for the customers, many of whom tipped him, and helping the old clerk stack cans and water vegetables and sweep out the floor. Soon he was working Friday afternoons as well as all day Saturday, and even Mr. Perc grudgingly admitted he was a help.

Not as part of his job but because he liked doing it, he usually showed up at the dock on the days old Mr. Gavin delivered to the lake people. Eddie helped load the boxes of groceries and cans of kerosene and cartons of pop and beer and listened to Mr. Gavin's stories about the old days. Mr. Gavin's wife was dead, and Eddie suspected nobody paid much attention when the old man felt like talking. He enjoyed Mr. Gavin's tales about his wild youth at Bates College, all the girls who were mad about him, the bootleg gin that tasted like battery acid and could turn your hair green.

Once in a while Mr. Gavin would ask about New York, but most of the time he wanted to talk about his own life. One day he said unexpectedly, "Are you an orphan?"

"No," Eddie said. "I'm a bastard."

Mr. Gavin's jaw dropped and his false teeth shifted a little. "I'll be blessed! I never heard a fella say that so cheerful before. Usually somebody *calls* him a bastard, and then there's a knock-down-drag-out fight."

Eddie shrugged. "Bastard or not, it's no skin off my nose."

"Where's your ma?"

"I don't know. She was never around. She isn't quite right in the head. Fawn and I don't know who our fathers

160

were, and we never missed 'em. Our grandmother brought us up better than any real parents could."

"Where's she now, your grandmother?"

"She died. Back in May."

"Oh." Mr. Gavin sat down on a box of groceries and stared at a pair of sea gulls who were fighting over a piece of garbage floating on the water. "Well, I'm sorry. She must have been a fine woman, 'cause you're a fine boy."

"Thank you." Eddie was surprised and touched. Mr. Gavin never got personal. "She was the best woman that ever lived. You and she would have hit it off fine."

"Liked a good story, did she?"

"Loved to hear 'em, loved to tell 'em."

Mr. Gavin shook his head. He relighted his pipe. "All the best ones are gone." Then he stood up suddenly, and for a moment he seemed shaky. "Well, time to get on my way."

Eddie held the bow. "You ever want me to go around with you and help you unload, you let me know."

"Oh, I can manage. That's the one thing they still let me do. You wouldn't think it was my store, the way they boss me around." He said that often. "It's no good gettin' old." He looked at Eddie and winked. "No future in it. You do a lot of work here, helping me load. You ought to let me pay you."

"I get paid at the store. I come down here because I like to listen to your stories."

Mr. Gavin grinned. "Always did like to brag. Well, here we go." He swung into the boat, Eddie pushed him out into the open water, and he got the motor going. He waved without looking back.

Eddie stood watching him. He hoped the people at the cottages helped him unload their stuff. Probably some did, some didn't. He kind of understood, though, why Mr. Gavin insisted on doing it alone. It was the only thing left that he was in charge of.

It was a Friday and he had an hour before he went to work. Fawn was over at the Terrys', learning to read, learning a little French, having lunch. He wandered up the street and went into Sandra's Spa to get a sandwich. It felt good to have money of his own. Stevie kept the accounts for all of them. She and Alex had worked out a system where each person paid his share according to his income. Eddie knew they had figured it out to let him off easy, but he tried to make up for it in other ways. Every Sunday afternoon now he and Mrs. Haines went fishing, and his share of the catch went into the family menu. Sometimes when Mr. Perc wasn't around, the old clerk, whose name was Georgie, slipped him some slightly wilted vegetables or cans that were dented a little. Alex said the dented cans would probably give them ptomaine, but so far they hadn't.

"Cheeseburger and a strawberry shake?" Sandra said.

"How'd you guess?" He always ordered them. He liked Sandra. She was a middle-aged bleached blond with a high voice and an endless line of chatter, but she was kind-hearted and funny.

"Been down helpin' the old man load up the boat?" She tossed the burger onto the grill, and for a moment he remembered that waitress in the place where they'd got bumped off the train, before they met Alex. He wondered if she'd got out of there and gone into computers, the way she'd said.

"He comes in here for coffee and toast every morning," Sandra said, "old Mr. Gavin does. Says his daughter-in-law makes the toast so hard, he can't bite it with his false teeth. Poor old guy. I remember him when he looked like an ad from the L.L. Bean catalog, always sporty, always neat and tidy. He's made a gold mine out of that store. Knew enough to keep it open seven days a week all winter, once the winter sports people started coming. Now that snotty son of his treats him like a doddering old fool, and believe me, he is not."

"I know that," Eddie said. "He talks to me."

"He speaks well of you." Sandra added more melted cheese to the sandwich and gave it to Eddie. "He likes you."

"Well, I like him."

"He was down to the legislature, must have been eight or ten years. That was a long time back, before Myra Haines's husband got elected."

"Did Mr. Perc Gavin go to college?"

"Perc? Nah. Perc nearly busted a gut getting through high school. The old man sent him to a fancy boarding school, Tilton, I think it was, but they kicked him out. Perc's brains are in his feet."

Eddie thought about that later in the afternoon, when Mr. Perc snarled at him to hurry up with the groceries. There were an unusually large number of customers, and

Eddie had to move fast to keep up. One of them was a man he didn't like, a retired lawyer who lived in a restored farmhouse on the edge of town. He wore mirror sunglasses and sporty clothes that were too young for him, and he was always in a hurry, although as far as Eddie could find out, he did nothing but putter around his expensive house and entertain friends from the city. He always wanted things like Beluga caviar and a special brand of pâté de foie gras, and although he had known for a long time that the store didn't carry them, he always made a fuss.

Eddie had carried out two heavy boxes to the man's late-model Thunderbird, being extra careful not to touch the paint, feeling the man's watchful eyes on him. Now he was carrying two large, heavy glass containers of the special springwater the man always demanded. Normally he would have taken one at a time down the steep wooden steps, but the lawyer was insisting that he hurry, as if Eddie had not already been hurrying as fast as he could.

Out of the corner of his eye he saw Bubber and two of his chums coming down the street on their bikes, jumping curbs, narrowly missing people on foot, doing wheelies to show off. He wanted them to get past the store before he got to the sidewalk because the heaviness of the water jugs and the descent of the steps gave him a momentum that would be hard to check.

He felt tired and irritated, and his back hurt from the weight. As he stepped off the bottom step onto the sidewalk, the lawyer right behind him, Bubber let out one of his famous cowboy yells and swerved skillfully so that

Eddie couldn't avoid crashing into the back wheel of the bike.

The impact didn't knock him down, but it threw him sideways, and the jug of water tore out of his right hand, crashing on the sidewalk and sending up a shower of springwater all over the lawyer's gabardine trousers.

The lawyer yelled. Bubber and his friends were already out of sight. Eddie stood, holding one jug, looking down at the smashed glass and the widening puddle of water that was now spotting the lawyer's eighty-dollar boat shoes.

Georgie and Mr. Perc were on the steps, Mr. Perc red-faced with horror and embarrassment at what had been done to one of his best customers.

The lawyer was talking so fast, in such a furious high voice, Eddie didn't even try to understand what he was saying.

"You're fired!" Mr. Perc yelled at Eddie. "Georgie, get Mr. Peyton another jug of water. On the house, sir, on us. And please send us the cleaning bill for your trousers." He was almost wringing his hands, and in spite of the desperation of the moment, it struck Eddie that he had never seen anyone really wring his hands before.

"It's only water," Georgie murmured, but he went inside and brought out another jug. Eddie took it from him and put it in the trunk of the car.

"You've cut your hand," Georgie said.

Eddie looked down at the blood oozing from the side of his hand, where the handle must have broken off.

"Move away!" The lawyer was still having a fit. "Don't get blood all over my car."

"Beat it," Mr. Perc said to Eddie. "You're fired. Leave." He opened the car door for the lawyer, apologizing all the way.

Eddie turned away, but as the lawyer drove off, Mr. Perc yelled at him. "Clean up that glass first."

"I'll do it," Georgie said. "You go over to Tom's and get your hand fixed. It wasn't your fault. That Bubber ought to be tarred and feathered and run out of town."

Feeling dazed at the speed of all that had happened, Eddie started down the street. Sandra came to her door.

"Eddie," she said, "come in. I'll fix your hand. I saw what happened. I'll have a thing or two to report to old Mr. Gavin, believe you me." She took him into a small office at the back of the store, examined the cut, washed it out, and carefully bandaged it. "It doesn't need stitches. It's just bloody, hit a vein. I was a Red Cross worker when I was young. I'm no surgeon but I can bandage a cut. You look pale. Sit here."

Gratefully Eddie sank back on the small sofa. He felt as if he was going to be sick. She gave him something bubbly in a small glass and made him lie down. "You just lie here till you feel better." She went out to wait on a customer.

Bubber, Eddie thought. Bubber. I'll get him for this.

 Chapter 24

EDDIE HAD NOT HAD MUCH TO SAY ABOUT LOSING HIS job, but Stevie had heard the story from several different people. Even Georgie had met her on the street and given her his eyewitness version. He was upset not only by the unfairness, but because he missed Eddie's help.

"The boss is too thick-skulled to admit he was wrong," he said. "Him and the old man had a terrible row about it. I thought the old man was going to have a stroke, he was so mad. But, like Perc reminded him, it's in the contract that Perc runs the store his way. Mr. G. should have known better than to let him get that kind of power." He looked over his shoulder. "Don't say I told you all this. I need my job."

"You know I won't. Eddie liked you a lot. He doesn't say much, but I know he feels bad. He feels like he failed at his very first job."

"Fail, nothing! He was the best little worker we ever had."

"Well, right now he's rebuilding Mrs. Haines's toolshed, so that's keeping him pretty busy."

"The boy is well liked," Georgie said. "Well liked." He nodded several times and scurried off down the street, his back curved, bald head thrust out, as if he might at any moment fall forward.

He's too old to be doing all the hard work he does in that store, Stevie thought. She would tell Eddie the nice things he said about him.

She went along the road to the library. It wasn't one of her weeding days, so she had promised to help Diana shelve books. Diana was comforting to be with. She listened sympathetically if Stevie felt like talking or just worked quietly if she didn't. Today Stevie didn't feel like talking. She had had a letter from her father that worried her. She knew he was dreading the thought of her coming to Alaska. The all-male, hardworking life he was living, in an atmosphere so different from any he had been used to, was a welcome change, helping him put behind the death of his wife and the loss of his farm. Having a fourteen-year-old daughter arrive was going to make a great difference. And he definitely didn't want Eddie and Fawn added to his responsibilities. She could understand that—he had no reason to feel any concern for them—but she was just as determined not to leave them. She did not want to go to Alaska. But if she didn't, she would have to find some alternative. If only she were a couple of years older, and able to take a real job.

She went into the library. Diana was checking out some books for the Reverend Fuller. He gave her his all-encompassing smile and took a step toward her as if to talk, but she picked up a pile of books and disappeared into the stacks. The Reverend asked too many questions.

Up the road at Mrs. Haines's place, Eddie aimed his hammer at the last nail on a clapboard, replacing one that had cracked. Thanks to Alex he had learned how to measure carefully and exactly, how to line up his material, how to bevel and countersink, words he had never even heard of till this summer. He liked carpentry, although not with the passion Alex had for it, not as a full-time job. He thought he might like to work as one of those engineers who did the sound for tapes and CDs. It sounded cool, listening to great groups make music.

He stood back and looked at the shed. Tomorrow he would paint the whole thing.

He put away his tools and cleaned up. He had worked all day and he was hot and tired. He'd go back to camp and have a swim, or at least a dip, not enough to break the "no swimming alone" rule. Fawn was at the Terrys'. She and Stevie would come home in the outboard with Alex. Eddie had come over alone in the canoe. Alex said he paddled the canoe and rowed the boat very well. Any praise, especially from Alex, was welcome after that mess about losing his job. He hadn't seen old Mr. Gavin since, but he had heard that the old man had had a big row with his son. He'd go down tomorrow and help him load the boat so Mr. Gavin wouldn't think Eddie held it against him that he was fired.

He took his time paddling back to camp. It was a hot,

still afternoon, and the sun made a glare on the water. The paddle blistered the palms of his hands. He was very brown from the days of sun, and he knew his muscles were in much better shape than they had been before. Gram used to worry about his not getting enough sunlight. She was always snapping up window shades. Gram would have liked New Hampshire, except there were no pastrami sandwiches.

He brought the canoe neatly alongside the dock, jumped out, pulled it clear of the water, turned it over, and put the paddles in the rec building. Alex said if they were here next summer, they'd build a boat house.

Next summer? Eddie didn't even know where'd he be next month. He kept trying to work out some plan, but everything he thought of had obstacles that he couldn't get around. He and Fawn could maybe stay right here, for instance, do a little winterizing on the rec building, buy a small stove. When the lake froze, they could walk around the lake path to school or even walk across the lake if the ice was thick enough. But grown-ups would stop them. They always did. They'd let runaway kids live on the streets in New York and hardly lift a hand to help them, but if a kid worked out a good safe plan like this one, they'd stop him cold. Maybe he should get in touch with the welfare here. It might be better than in New York. He hated the idea, but sooner or later he had to do something.

He knew good and well Stevie's father wasn't going to take them to live with him in Alaska. Why should he? The less Stevie talked about the future, the more worried he knew she was, worried about Fawn and him. After all she'd done, she shouldn't have to worry about them anymore. He'd *have* to think of something. If the worst came to the absolute worst, he could go back to New York and leave Fawn here. He knew the Terrys or maybe Mrs. Haines would look after her. They loved her.

He changed into his swim trunks and waded into the cove. The water was cold, but it felt good. He went out to shoulder depth and swam back to shore in a couple of strokes, then did it again and again. He longed to go for a real swim, but rules were rules, and he knew this one made sense. A person could get a cramp and drown, no matter how good a swimmer he was.

After a while he went over to the dock and lay down on his bath towel, facedown, enjoying the warm sun on his back. Pretty soon he would get up and start fixing supper for the gang. Maybe he'd make a big three-bean salad. Stevie had developed a passion for garbanzos, which she'd never heard of till he brought some home from Gavins'. He hadn't been in the store since they fired him.

He moved a little as the sunlight shifted. What else for supper? He could toast a can of brown bread if he made a small fire. By supper time the day would cool off. You could feel autumn in the nights now.

All right, three-bean salad, brown bread, Mr. Mason's pears, milk for Fawn if Stevie remembered to bring some, coffee for the rest of them. He had promoted himself to the ranks of coffee drinkers when he became thirteen. Alex said it would stunt his growth, but he knew he was kidding.

He heard the faint splash of oars, not bothering to look up. There were often boats on the lake now that all the summer cottages were full. Some young guy down where he and Mrs. Haines fished had a catamaran with striped sails that was a real beauty. On a breezy day it was like watching a rainbow skim across the lake.

The sound of oars had stopped. He turned his head, but he didn't see anyone. Probably the Currans, whose cottage was the nearest.

He heard twigs crackle somewhere along the path from the tents, but still he was too relaxed to look up. Maybe it was the golden retriever who sometimes came by to visit.

He stretched out his arms. The muscles in his shoulders ached from holding the clapboards in place while he nailed them up. Muscles were always hurting where you didn't even know you had any.

"*Yah!*" It was a loud bellow, close to him.

He leaped to his feet. He saw the rowboat close to shore, Bubber's friend shipping the oars and watching him, and he saw Bubber coming toward him on the dock, flapping his arms and waving the mezuzah as if he were about to hurl it into the lake.

Chapter 25

"YAH, YAH, YAH!" BUBBER DID A CLUMSY LITTLE dance and pulled his arm back in a throwing motion.

"Put that down." Eddie's voice was low. The muscles in his stomach felt like tight knots. The sight of his grandmother's beloved mezuzah in Bubber's fat sweaty fist made the blood pound in his ears.

"Try and make me," Bubber taunted. He moved sideways along the edge of the dock. Slowly Eddie circled until their positions were almost reversed, Bubber with his back to the lake.

The boy in the boat called, "What you got, Bub?"

"It was hangin' on his tent. Looks like a penny whistle." He put one end of it to his mouth.

"If you don't put that down, I'll kill you."

Bubber blinked. Something in Eddie's tone was more frightening than the usual threats. "It ain't any good," he said. He aimed it at the water again, but he didn't throw it.

The mezuzah in Bubber's possession, the job Bubber had made him lose, the names Bubber had called him, the anti-Semitic taunts, all of it suddenly rose in Eddie's throat like vomit. He sprang at Bubber and grabbed the sides of his floppy shirt and pulled them up over Bubber's head, pinning his arms.

The mezuzah fell to the dock. Eddie rammed his knee into Bubber's stomach and shoved him backward. Bubber sailed off the dock into the lake with a splash that rocked his friend's rowboat. Bubber sank out of sight, and the boy in the boat began frantically to row away.

Breathing hard, Eddie picked up the mezuzah, carefully brushed it off, and took it into the rec building. He laid it on the table and came out again.

Bubber surfaced, struggling to get free of the cloth clinging to his head. He couldn't get his arms out of the shirt that stuck to him like a shroud. Eddie stood on the end of the dock and watched him. The boy in the boat was halfway across the lake, rowing in fast, choppy, panicky strokes. One of his oars skittered along the top of the water and nearly threw him over backward. Eddie laughed.

Bubber went down again. Eddie watched the bubbles and ripples in the water. He felt tired and empty but calm, like that time when he had the flu and was out of his head, and then the fever broke and he just felt detached from everything.

He'd better do something about Bubber. He couldn't just let him drown. He jumped off the dock into the deep water. Bubber looked like a big fish under the water. One arm was free, and he was clawing at the cloth and kicking his feet.

Eddie grabbed the shirt and pulled the squirming Bubber to the surface. Once he had to let go as Bubber swung out his arm and hit Eddie in the face. He got hold of him again, tried to get him in the lifesaving grip that Alex had shown him, but he ended up ramming him against the dock shoulder first.

Bubber grabbed at the dock with his free hand. Eddie climbed out, seized Bubber by the seat of his pants, and hauled him out of the water, then went and sat down in one of the dock chairs, out of breath.

Bubber lay on his stomach on the dock, heaving and gasping, spitting up water, groaning. Like a beached whale, Eddie thought. Finally Bubber pulled himself to his knees, choked and coughed, swayed and almost fell over again. Then with a mighty effort he got to his feet, his eyes glazed. Swinging his head back and forth like a punchy prizefighter, he lurched toward Eddie.

Eddie stood up and shoved Bubber into the other chair.

"You tried to drown me." Bubber's voice sounded hollow, with gurgles in it.

"Oh, don't be an ass," Eddie said wearily. "Who pulled you out? Your friend went off and left you so fast, he burned holes in the lake."

Bubber looked out at the lake. The boat was not in sight. "How'm I gonna get home?"

"Walk," Eddie said. "You can walk on water, can't you, Bubber? A superman like you?"

"I feel sick," Bubber said. "My heart's bumping."

Eddie got up and went over to the cove where they kept their refrigerated box in the water. He brought back two Cokes and gave one to Bubber.

Bubber held it in shaking hands. He couldn't manage the top. Eddie gave him his own opened bottle and took the other one.

"I know you got that switchblade," Bubber said. "You gonna cut me?"

"What switchblade?"

"You know."

"Oh, drink your Coke and shut up."

A squirrel ran across the dock, and Bubber jumped as if it were a charging tiger. Eddie watched him. Bubber was afraid of him. It should have felt good, but the thing that was on his mind was that if he had had his knife at the moment when Bubber put his filthy mouth on Gram's mezuzah, he would have cut him. Thanks, GRAM7, he thought. I'm glad it's at the bottom of the lake.

"Why do you let them call you Bubber?" he said.

Bubber looked blank. He took a long drink of the Coke. "That's my nickname."

"It's not much of a nickname. Do you like it? It sounds like a two-year-old, a blubbery, sickening, two-year-old brat."

"Don't you talk to me like that," Bubber said, but his heart wasn't in it. There was a long pause, and then he said, "I don't like it."

"What's your real name?"

"Fred."

"You're going to have to walk home, Fred. It's three miles, and it's hot, and the mosquitoes are fierce, but it's the only way you can get there."

Bubber looked horrified. "I can't walk three miles. It's too hot. You can take me home in your canoe."

"Why should I do that?"

Bubber stared at him and then at his own Coke. "I'll pay you."

"It's not a taxi."

Bubber finished his Coke and dropped the bottle on the dock. It rolled almost to the water's edge.

"Pick that up," Eddie said. "This is not the town dump."

"I will not."

"Pick it up, Fred." He made a motion with his hand.

"Where do you keep your knife?" Bubber said.

"In a good place."

Bubber hoisted himself out of the chair and put the bottle on the table.

"Now go on home. And Fred, don't ever mess with me again."

Bubber gave him a long look. Then he lumbered off along the path toward town.

Chapter 26

EDDIE DECIDED NOT TO TELL THE OTHERS ABOUT BUB-
ber. Or Fred, as he was trying to think of him now. If
they heard about it in town, he'd tell them, but he had
an idea that Fred wasn't going to be spreading it around.

The next day he had Mrs. Haines's tool shed to paint,
and it was a good cool day for it. While he was there, he
took a look in the Berlin-area phone book, but there wasn't
anything listed under *welfare*. Maybe it was adoption agen-
cies he should be looking for. He'd need to find out more
about what he should do.

Gram had never had anything to do with welfare. She'd
had Social Security and Gramps's insurance money, and
she had made do. She didn't believe in banks. He remembered the bunch of envelopes she kept in the china closet;
one said Rent, one said Grocs., one said Children, and
one said Misc. She figured out to a penny how much to
save for their needs. When Gram died, his mother found
the envelopes and grabbed whatever cash was left.

He sighed and gently removed the caterpillar that had

178

fallen down the side of the shed and stuck in the wet paint. He didn't really like to paint, but he did it carefully so Mrs. Haines would be pleased.

She always left him sandwiches and milk in the kitchen for lunch and usually a candy bar or ice cream. At noon he got the paint off his hands with a turpentine-soaked rag, went into the house, and washed in the kitchen sink.

Stevie and Fawn had gone to North Conway with Alex to get some special kind of wood that Tom needed. Later they were all going to have a barbecue at the Terrys', the librarian and the cop, too, the same bunch that had been here on the Fourth. Mrs. Haines said the cop had taken the librarian to the county fair. Maybe they'd fall in love or something.

When he came out after his lunch, Fred rode up on his bike. He was alone. He rode into the yard. "Hi," he said.

"Hi, Fred."

"What you doin'?"

"Painting the shed." Eddie went back to work, and Fred sat on his bike watching him.

"You tell anybody about what happened yesterday?"

"Nope."

"Me neither. I told Jerry I lost my balance and fell in the lake and you pulled me out. I told him if he talked about it, I'd tell everybody in town how he rowed off without helping me."

"Yeah." Eddie wished Fred would go away. He didn't feel like conversation, especially with Fred.

"I wanted to ask you, that thing that I grabbed off your tent, that wasn't a penny whistle, was it?"

179

"No."

"What is it? Jerry said it's a pipe for smoking crack."

Eddie sighed. "It's called a mezuzah. It's a Jewish religious symbol."

"Oh. Is there something inside?"

Eddie painted a place over the door before he answered. How did you explain things to idiots? "Do you know what parchment is?" He didn't wait for an answer. "It used to be sheepskin or goatskin, treated so you could write on it. Now it's a special kind of paper that looks like that."

"What's written on it? Is it like a curse or anything?"

"It's from Deuteronomy, in the Torah. Your Bible."

"*My* Bible?" Fred looked stunned.

"Well, everybody's. 'Hear, O Israel, the Lord our God is one Lord: And thou shalt love the Lord the God with all thine heart, and with all they soul, and with all thy might . . .' " He stopped, hearing Gram's voice reading the words. Tears filled his eyes, and he turned his head away.

"That's the kind of stuff they say in *our* church," Fred said, as if he couldn't believe it. "Jerry told me it was curses and devil stuff that Jews believe in—"

Eddie interrupted him fiercely. "Oh, shut up, Fred, and scram out of here, will you? I'm busy."

"Sure, okay." Fred turned his bike around. "Man, is Jerry going to be surprised. Wait till I tell him—'Wrong as usual, Jerry.' " He rode off down the drive, weaving from one side to the other in wide loops.

Eddie thought of a line he had always remembered from *Black Beauty*—it had struck him again when he read the

180

book to Fawn—something about ignorance being almost as bad as wickedness. He wiped his face with the back of his hand and went at his painting with so much energy, he was just finishing when Mrs. Haines came home.

"Eddie! I thought that was a two-day job. Come on in and have some iced coffee with vanilla ice cream in it. How does that grab you?"

He took a shower while Mrs. Haines was making the coffee, and she gave him a pair of white shorts and a navy blue sweatshirt that had belonged to her youngest boy. "I never throw anything away," she said. "The boys tease me about it, but see, things come in handy when you least expect it." She tossed his own clothes into the washing machine.

When they were sitting at the kitchen table with their iced coffee, she said, "I talked to all of my kids today. My telephone bill is going to be enormous. But it was wonderful. I even heard the new baby in Hawaii belch, loud and clear, all the way across the Pacific Ocean and the continent of America. Isn't science wonderful?"

"Do you always call them all at once?" Eddie said.

"No. I had something to talk over with them. They are a lovely lot of people, if I do say so. It's lonesome without them."

Later when they arrived at the Terrys', Alex and Stevie and Fawn had just come back.

"There's snow on top of Mount Washington," Fawn told Eddie. "Can we learn to ski next winter, Eddie?"

"We'll see."

It was a great barbecue and everybody was in good

spirits, except Eddie, who couldn't shake his depression. He ought to try to enjoy the good times while they were here, but his mind kept slipping ahead to the future. What if they couldn't find a foster home for the two of them? What if the foster parents were mean to Fawn when he wasn't around? What if he never saw Stevie again? Or Alex or Mrs. Haines or the Terrys, but especially Stevie? If she went to Alaska, she might as well go to the moon.

Miss Diana, the librarian, commented on Eddie's quietness. "You're as silent as people tell me I am, Eddie. Everything all right?"

"Sure. Fine." He gave her his best smile. "You look real nice in that pink sweater." He noticed that Joe McCord obviously thought so, too. He wondered if he'd ever fall in love and look at some girl in that goofy way.

He heard Mrs. Haines ask Stevie for the phone number in Alaska where they had called her father. Stevie got it for her from her wallet. He could see that Stevie was puzzled, but Mrs. Haines didn't explain. Stevie was wearing her mother's red cashmere sweater. He wondered if Stevie's mother and Gram and Mrs. Haines's husband were sitting around having coffee and kichel and watching them.

Fawn climbed into Mrs. Haines's lap and said slowly and carefully, *"Je vous aime."*

Mrs. Haines hugged her. "I love you, too, Fawn. Your accent is much better than mine."

"All I remember from high-school French," Joe McCoy said, "is a rhyme that goes *'Je vous aime, Je vous adore, que voulez vous de plus encore?'* " He grinned at Diana, and she smiled back at him.

"What's it mean?" Eddie said, although he had a pretty good idea it was about love.

Annette said, " 'I love you, I adore you, what more do you want?' "

Eddie laughed. That was a good one. He'd have to remember it. He looked at Stevie and saw the expression on her face as she gazed at Alex, who was fiddling with the coals in the barbecue. Oh no! Not Stevie in love with Alex! And Joe in love with Diana, and Fawn in love with Mrs. Haines, and Annette and Tom still in love with each other after all these years? Bring on the violins.

"Friends," he said, "this is your FM station LOVE. Jascha Rabinowitz, the famous violinist, will now play 'Love, Your Magic Spell Is Everywhere.' Stay tuned."

Chapter 17

THE LAKE WAS A BIT CHOPPY FOR FISHING, BUT EDDIE and Mrs. Haines rowed down to their favorite spot, a cove at the eastern end of the lake. Eddie had meant to get up early and go to the village to help Mr. Gavin load his boat. He made excuses for himself, but in his heart he knew he had been avoiding Mr. Gavin because he was afraid that he was disappointed in him for losing his job.

A couple of times he had seen him sitting on his chair tilted back against the front of the store, and they had waved to each other, Mr. Gavin with his stiff little salute, but they hadn't talked. He thought Mr. Gavin looked unwell.

Mrs. Haines picked up the pole to push off when the boat drifted too close to shore. "When you grow up and go to Oxford as a Rhodes scholar, you'll float down the river with a beautiful English girl in a punt, using a pole like this."

"I get the picture," Eddie said. "And just as I'm about

184

to make a pass at her, she'll land a fish and it'll hit me in the face, and there goes another beautiful romance."

Mrs. Haines chuckled. "I don't think they fish from punts."

"What are they for, then?"

"Beautiful romance." She baited her line and cast it over the side. "Do you miss New York, Eddie?"

Eddie had finally learned to put a worm on a hook without feeling sick. "Sure, in lots of ways. But it's no place for Fawn to be."

She looked at him over the tops of her dark glasses. "Where do you want to be? If you had your choice."

He wished she wouldn't spoil this nice afternoon. "Right here the way things are, I guess. But that's impossible." For a moment he was tempted to ask her if she knew any welfare or foster-home people, but if he did, she'd take it on as her responsibility, and it wasn't. It was his. "Alex caught an eel the other day, and he cooked it and ate it! Yuk!"

"Eels are delicious."

"They look like snakes to me."

"People eat snakes. Canned rattlesnake meat is a delicacy, very expensive."

"The eel jumped in the pan while it was cooking."

"That's just a reflex. It wasn't alive."

Eddie pointed to the catamaran with the colored sails, racing with the wind. "I'd like to have me one of those."

She watched the beautiful boat with a faraway look. He wondered what she was thinking about.

She jerked to attention at a tug on her line. Playing the line skillfully for a few minutes, she landed a good-sized trout.

"Nice one." Eddie closed his eyes as she bopped it on the back of the head to kill it and put it in her creel. He knew that it was better to kill them at once than to let them lie there without air, gasping and flopping, but still he hated to watch. She killed his for him without his asking her to.

She rebaited her line and pushed the boat a little further out, till the pole wouldn't touch bottom. The sound of an outboard reached them before the boat came into sight.

"Mr. Gavin," Eddie said. "I should have gone over and helped him load."

Idly they watched his boat chug into the docks of the cottages where he had deliveries to make. Eddie was relieved to see that in each place someone came down to meet him and help unload.

"Look!" Mrs. Haines pointed to the other side of their boat. A school of sunfish danced through the water like flying gold and copper and green discs. Eddie pulled back his line so they wouldn't get caught.

"They're good eating, you know," Mrs. Haines said, "though you have to be careful to get all those spines out."

"They're too pretty to catch," Eddie said.

A few minutes later he caught a bass, and then almost as soon as he threw his line in again, a pickerel about two feet long.

"A beauty!" The creel, lined with wet leaves, was almost full now. Mrs. Haines rowed out further into the lake.

186

Mr. Gavin's boat had come around and was starting up their side. Eddie hoped he'd stop to talk for a minute.

The old outboard was heading in toward the camp where the golden retriever lived. Eddie moved the creel a little so he could stretch his legs. When he looked up, he gasped. Mr. Gavin was running his boat straight at the shore, not slowing down at all. At the last moment the boat swerved around and came out into open water, heading straight for them, going as fast as the old motor would take it.

Mrs. Haines was bent over, adjusting the oarlock. Eddie tried to yell but no sound came out of his mouth. Mr Gavin was slumped down in his boat, his head on his chest. He was going to crash into them.

"What's all that racket?" Mrs. Haines started to turn, and her mouth opened in alarm as she saw Mr. Gavin's boat driving through the choppy water directly at them.

Eddie grabbed the oar nearest to him and rowed with all his strength to move out of Mr. Gavin's path.

The bow of the old outboard hit the rowboat a glancing blow that almost overturned it, then veered around sharply and headed for a tiny beach not far from another cottage. It never slowed down.

As they struggled to keep their own boat from overturning in the wash of the motorboat, they heard the crash as it ran full speed onto the shore. The moment of silence when the outboard stopped was painful.

The impact threw Mr. Gavin onto the strip of sand where he lay still. The golden retriever came running along the shore, barking, and behind him the couple who owned him ran toward the wreck of the boat.

Mrs. Haines grabbed the other oar, and she and Eddie pulled toward shore. When they were in shallow water, Mrs. Haines climbed out and waded ashore. Eddie brought the boat in and jumped out.

The man from the cottage was kneeling beside Mr. Gavin. He looked up at Mrs. Haines.

"It's old Mr. Gavin," he said. "He's dead."

Chapter 28

THE LITTLE CHURCH WAS FULL, WITH PEOPLE STANDING at the back. Nearly every adult in North Lakeville was there, and most of the summer people from the cottages.

Eddie was sitting with Alex and Mrs. Haines and the Terrys. Stevie had taken Fawn on a picnic. Eddie had explained to Fawn that old Mr. Gavin had died, had had a stroke and smashed up his boat, but he didn't want her to go to the funeral. She was too young, and it was too soon after Gram's death. He wished he didn't have to be there himself, although at the same time he would not have stayed away for anything.

Mr. Gavin's son and daughter-in-law and the three grandchildren sat stiff and expressionless in the front row as the Reverend Fuller prayed and talked for a long time. It got very hot in the crowded church, and for a terrible moment Eddie thought he was going to faint. Everything seemed to be whirling around, and he couldn't focus his eyes.

Mrs. Haines noticed and pushed his head down between

189

his knees. After a minute he felt better, hoping no one had seen him. Annette, on the other side of him, held his hand for a minute, and he closed his eyes, comforted by the cool, strong grip.

When the pallbearers carried Mr. Gavin's casket down the aisle, close to Eddie, he almost expected Mr. Gavin to shove at the lid, sit up, and tell one of his wonderful stories.

Mrs. Haines had to get back to the post office for the afternoon mail, and Alex went back to work at Tom's, but Eddie walked the half mile to the cemetery. Most of the people in the church had gone home. Eddie stood back at the edge of the group that had come to the grave. He wished he had helped Mr. Gavin load his boat that day. He might have noticed that he wasn't well and kept him from going out on his rounds. On the other hand, if Mr. Gavin had his druthers, as he would say, Eddie was sure he would rather have died in his boat, making his rounds, than in bed at home or in a hospital.

The daughter-in-law and the youngest grandson were crying now. A man, a stranger to Eddie, got out of a blue Mercedes 300SL and stood near Eddie. He was wearing an expensive-looking suit and sunglasses. He was oldish, maybe as old as Mr. Gavin, although he looked healthier. He glanced at Eddie, but he didn't speak to anyone. His car had Maine plates.

The men lowering the casket into the grave were making a bad job of it. It slipped and almost got away from them. Eddie heard the man near him say something sharp under his breath.

Finally they managed it, and the Reverend Fuller said some words that were lost in the wind before they reached Eddie. He wasn't listening anyway. Tears were streaming down his face. He knew he was crying as much for Gram as for Mr. Gavin. He thought of the crazy little vision he'd had the other night of Gram and Mr. Haines and Stevie's mother having coffee and heavenly kichel together, watching over their people. Now Mr. Gavin could sit down with them. Happy knishes, Mr. Gavin.

The service was over. The man with the Mercedes started to leave, then turned to Eddie. "You a relative?"

Eddie wiped the tears away with his sleeve. "No, sir. I just liked him a lot. He used to tell me stories about when he was young."

"He was my college roommate," the man said.

Eddie's eyes widened. "No kidding! Oh, that's great. I wish he knew you were here."

"Who knows? Maybe he does. Did he tell you how wild we were in college?"

"He sure did."

"Did he tell you about the time we tied a dead skunk to the flagpole in front of the town hall?"

Eddie smiled. "I think he forgot to tell me that one."

The man was moving toward his car, keeping an eye on Mr. Perc Gavin, as if he wanted to avoid him. "My name is Bart Cronin. I've got a little inn over to Bar Harbor." He took a card out of its case, scribbled his name on the back, and gave it to Eddie. "Any time you're over that way, drop in and have a lobster on the house. Any friend of Gav's is a friend of mine."

"Thank you. I sure will."

The man got behind the wheel of the Mercedes and drove off just as Perc came up. "Was that Bart Cronin?" he said in his suspicious way.

"That's what he said."

"You'd think he could have offered condolences."

"He came clear from Bar Harbor." Eddie turned to go.

"Hold on," Perc said. "Stop in the store tomorrow morning. I've got something for you."

"All right." Eddie assumed it was the last day's pay, which he never had collected. "I'm sorry about your father."

Perc gave him an ungracious nod. "He was an old man."

Eddie walked away. He longed to say, He wasn't anywhere near as old as you are.

Chapter 29

Mrs. HAINES HAD ASKED ALEX AND EDDIE AND FAWN and Stevie to come to supper. It was important, she said. No one else was coming, not even the Terrys, although they knew about it.

Mrs. Haines had bought some Maine lobsters that she stuffed and baked. Stevie thought she could safely say it was the best thing she had ever eaten in her whole life. She did, in fact, say so, several times. Nobody disagreed.

During the meal Mrs. Haines seemed unusually quiet, almost nervous. Stevie watched her, wondering what was bothering her. Perhaps Mr. Gavin's death had made her think too much about her husband's death. He, too, had died of a stroke, quite a lot younger than Mr. Gavin. She could see that the funeral had been hard on Eddie, too. She was glad that Fawn had given her a reason not to go.

From time to time they had all been giving Eddie delayed birthday presents. She had given him a fancy fishing rod of his own, just as good as Alex's. Alex had given him a Swiss army knife: "A tool," he had said to Eddie, "not a weapon." They both had noticed that Eddie's switchblade seemed to have disappeared, but no one mentioned it to him.

Tonight when they finished supper Mrs. Haines gave him her present, which had taken a while to come from Boston. It was a world-band radio that brought in stations from all over the globe. Eddie was ecstatic. Watching his face, Stevie thought, I'm glad they came to New Hampshire with me. But what will happen to us all?

Then Mrs. Haines gathered them in the living room, saw that they were comfortable, and said, "I have something to tell you. To ask you, really." She paused, looking uncharacteristically hesitant.

"So ask," Eddie said.

Stevie glanced at Alex. He knows, she thought, whatever it is.

"I've been doing a tremendous amount of telephoning and writing lately," Mrs. Haines said. "To my children, my lawyer, my accountant, to Stevie's father, to the welfare women over to Berlin. My ear is positively callused from all that phoning."

"What about?" Eddie looked alarmed.

Stevie was beginning to get a faint premonition. Only it couldn't be; it would be too good to be true.

"I didn't want to go off half-cocked," Mrs. Haines said. "My family claims I'm impulsive."

Fawn got up and sat in Mrs. Haines's lap. "*Je vous aime*," she said.

"Fawn, what a ham you are," Eddie said. "Don't steal this scene."

194

Mrs. Haines laughed and hugged Fawn. "I'm stalling because what if you say no?"

"Mrs. H!" Eddie said. "Cut the suspense!"

"When Alex goes to his boat school, to Maine, I would like you children to come and live with me." She said it fast and then leaned back in the chair.

No one spoke for a minute, and she began to look alarmed.

"You mean—not just for a week or two?" Stevie said.

"I mean forever. Your father didn't say yes to forever but he said yes for now."

"Live here?" Eddie's voice sounded faint.

She leaned forward again anxiously. "There's still red tape to work out. We have to locate your mother and get her okay."

"I'll find her," Eddie said. "I know who she hangs out with. And she'll celebrate for a month to get rid of us." He grabbed Fawn off Mrs. Haines's lap and swung her around the room. Suddenly he stopped. "Do I have to weed the garden?"

"*I'll* weed the garden," Stevie said. "You'd pull up all the vegetables." She didn't have to go to Alaska! She didn't have to figure out what to do with Eddie and Fawn. Alex would be gone, but not for long, and he would be back.

"Hold it, everybody." Alex was standing, aiming his camera at them. "Don't move." There was a click and a flash. "Got it."

Eddie grabbed his new radio and turned it on. A clear voice said, "*Hyvaa huomenta, nimeni on Eero Kokanon se Helsinki, Suomi. . . Kello on puoli seitseman.*"

195

"I couldn't have said it better," Eddie said.

Mrs. Haines wiped tears of laughter from her eyes. "You'll have to start calling me Myra," she said. "I can't have my own family calling me Mrs. Haines. It sounds like Jane Austen. Oh, thank God this house won't rattle around me like an empty dishpan any longer."

Across the room Stevie caught Eddie's eye. He held up his hand, making a circle of his thumb and forefinger. "Stay tuned," he said.

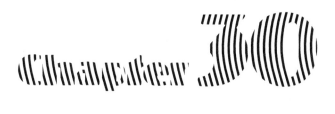

Chapter 30

IN THE MORNING EDDIE PADDLED THE CANOE TO THE village and went to get his pay or whatever it was Mr. Perc had for him.

Mr. Perc was sitting at his ancient rolltop desk that had probably been there since the store opened in 1905 He was looking sour as usual. "Georgie says I owe you for that last day," he said. He gave Eddie an envelope with some money in it. "You worked six hours and forty-five minutes. You'll find the pay corresponds."

"Thank you." Eddie put it in his pocket and turned to go.

"Aren't you going to count it?"

"Not right now."

"You'll never get ahead that way. Well, it's not my problem. Hold on a minute." He picked up a legal-size manila envelope sealed with a notary's stamp on the back. "This was among my father's effects. It has your name on it. God knows what's in it. He wouldn't tell *me*, of course." Mr. Perc sneezed and blew his nose on a maxi-sized tissue.

"Some trinket he wanted you to have, I suppose. Well," he said impatiently as Eddie stood looking at the envelope, "that's all. I'm a busy man."

Eddie left, stopping a moment to speak to Georgie and to Elsie, the checker. He walked slowly down to the public dock and sat on the edge, his feet hanging over, just above the water. The pay he put in his back pocket so he wouldn't accidentally drop it. If he knew Mr. Perc, it would be accurate to the penny.

The other envelope puzzled him. On the front in carefully printed letters it read *For Edward Sanders, in case of my death*. It was signed by Jason Percival Gavin and dated with the name of the town and county filled in. In the left-hand corner it said *Witnessed this day July 8, 1990*, and the signatures were those of George Walcott Mac-Pherson and Sandra Jones Folsom.

He broke the seal carefully, trying not to tear the envelope, and took out what was inside. A small green note was stuck to something that looked official. The little green slip of paper said: *Don't forget the stories. Yr friend, J. P. Gavin.*

Eddie opened the document. It was a five-hundred-dollar savings bond. He read every word on it and examined the design. Then he carefully put it back in the envelope with the green slip of paper. He sat there for a long time. The man who owned the gas station came down and took out his motorboat and said hi to Eddie.

He watched the gulls circling and diving and squawking in their harsh voices. He noticed the rainbow colors of a small oil leak from somebody's boat swirling in a slowly widening circle.

ED to GRAM, do you read me?

Loud and clear, Eddie. Over to you.

I guess it's like you always said: Keep a stiff upper lip and keep your eye peeled, and who knows, things may turn out all right. Part of the time anyway. I'll be in touch, Gram. Stay tuned.